The Boy Land Boomer

Ralph Bonehill

Contents

THE BOY LAND BOOMER

BY

Ralph Bonehill

PREFACE.

The Boy Land Boomer relates the adventures of a lad who, with his father, joins a number of daring men in an attempt to occupy the rich farming lands of Oklahoma before the time when that section of our country was thrown open to settlement under the homestead act.

Oklahoma consists of a tract of land which formerly formed a portion of the Indian Territory. This region was much in dispute as early as 1884 and 1885, when Captain "Oklahoma" Payne and Captain Couch did their best to force an entrance for the boomers under them. Boomers remained in the neighborhood for years, and another attempt was made to settle Oklahoma in 1886, and up to 1889, when, on April 22, the land was thrown open to settlement by a proclamation of the President. The mad rush to gain the best claims followed, and some of these scenes are related in the present volume.

The boomers, who numbered thousands, had among them several daring and well-known leaders, but not one was better known or more daring than the leader who is known in these pages as Pawnee Brown. This man was not alone a great Indian scout and hunter, but also one who had lived much among the Indians, could speak their language, and who had on several occasions acted as interpreter for the Government. He was well beloved by his followers, who relied upon his judgment in all things.

To some it may seem that the scenes in this book are overdrawn. Such, however, is not the fact. There was much of roughness in those days, and the author has continually found it necessary to tone down rather than to exaggerate in penning these scenes from real life.

CAPTAIN RALPH BONEHILL.

CHAPTER I.
DICK ARBUCKLE'S DISCOVERY.

F ather!"

The call came from a boy of sixteen, a bright, manly chap, who had just awakened from an unusually sound sleep in the rear end of a monstrous boomer's wagon.

The scene was upon the outskirts of Arkansas City, situated near the southern boundary line of Kansas and not many miles from the Oklahoma portion of the Indian Territory.

For weeks the city had been filling up with boomers on their way to pre-empt land within the confines of Oklahoma as soon as it became possible to do so.

The land in Oklahoma had for years been in dispute. Pioneers claimed the right to go in and stake out homesteads, but the soldiers of our government would not allow them to do so.

The secret of the matter was that the cattle kings of that section controlled everything, and as the grazing land of the territory was worth hundreds of thousands of dollars to them they fought desperately to keep the pioneers out, delaying, in every manner possible, legislation which tended to make the section an absolutely free one to would-be settlers.

But now the pioneers, or boomers as they were commonly called, were tired of waiting for the passage of a law which they knew must come sooner or later, and they intended to go ahead without legal authority.

It was a dark, tempestuous night, with the wind blowing fiercely and the rain coming down at irregular intervals. On the grassy plain were huddled the wagons, animals and trappings of over two hundred boomers. Here and there flared up the remains of a campfire, but the wind was blowing too strongly for these to be replenished, and the men had followed their wives and children into the big, canvas-covered wagons, to make themselves as comfortable as the crowded space permitted.

It was the rattle of the rain on the canvas covering of the wagon which had aroused the boy.

"I say father!" he repeated. "Father!"

Again there was no reply, and, kicking aside the blanket with which he had been covered, Dick Arbuckle clambered over some boxes piled high in the center of the vehicle to where he had left his parent resting less than three hours before.

"Gone!" cried the lad in astonishment. "What can this mean? What could take him outside in such a storm as this? Father!"

He now crawled to the opening at the front of the wagon and called at the top of his voice. Only the shrieking of the wind answered him. A dozen times he cried out, then paused to strike a somewhat damp match and light a smoky lantern hanging to the front ashen bow of the turn-out's covering. Holding the light over his head he peered forth into the inky darkness surrounding the boomer's temporary camp.

"Not a soul in sight," he mused. "It must be about midnight. Can something have happened to father? He said he felt rather strange in his head when he went to bed. If only Jack Rasco would come back."

From the front end of the wagon Dick Arbuckle shifted back to the rear. Here the same dreary outlook of storm, mud and flapping canvases presented itself. Not so much as a stray dog was in sight, and the nearest wagon was twenty feet away.

"I must find out where he is. Something is wrong, I feel certain of it."

Thus muttering to himself the youth hunted up his overcoat and hat, put them on, and, lantern in hand, swung himself into the sea of half-submerged prairie grass, and stalked over to the other wagon just mentioned.

"Mike Delaney!" he cried, kicking on the wagon wheel with the toe of his boot; "Mike Delaney, have you seen my father anywhere?"

"Sure, an' Moike Delaney is not here, Dick Arbuckle," came in a female voice. "He's gone off wid Pawnee Brown, and there's no tellin' whin he'll be back. Is yer father gone?"

"Yes, and I don't know where," and now Dick stepped closer, as the round and freckled face of Rosy Delaney peered forth from a hole in the canvas end. "He went to bed when I did, and now he's missing."

"Saints preserve us! Mebbe the Injuns scalped him now, Dick!" came in a voice full of terror.

"There are no Indians around here, Mrs. Delaney," answered the youth, half inclined to laugh. "But he's missing, and it's mighty strange, to say the least."

"He was sick, too, wasn't he?"

"Father hasn't been real well for a year. He left New York very largely in the hope that this climate would do him some good."

"Moike was sayin' his head throubles him a good bit."

"So it does, and that's why I am so worried. When he gets those awful pains he is apt to walk away and keep right on without knowing where he is going."

"Poor mon! Oi wisht Oi could help yez. Mebbe Moike will be back soon. Ain't Jack Rasco about?"

"No, he is off with Pawnee Brown, too. Rasco and Brown have been looking over the trails leading to Oklahoma. They are bound to outwit the United States cavalry, for the boomers have more right to that land than the cattle kings, and right is always might in the end."

"Especially wid Pawnee on the end o' it, Dick. He's a great mon, is Pawnee, only it do be afther givin' me the shivers to hear him spake the Pawnee language loike he was a rale Injun. Such a foine scout as he is has no roight to spake such a dirthy tongue. How illegant it would be now if he could spake rale Oirish."

"His knowledge of the Indian tongue has helped both him and our government a good deal, Mrs. Delaney. But I mustn't stop here talking. If my father----"

A wild, unearthly shriek cut short further talk upon Dick Arbuckle's part. It came from the darkness back of the camp and caused Mrs. Delaney to draw back and tumble to the bottom of her house on wheels in terror.

"It's the Banshee----" she began, when Dick interrupted her.

"It's Pumpkin Bill. I'd know his voice a mile off," he declared. "Somebody ought to send him back to where he belongs. Creation, what a racket!"

Nearer and nearer came the voice, rising and falling with the wind. The shrill shrieking penetrated to every wagon, and head after head was thrust out of the canvases to see what it meant. In another minute Pumpkin Bill, the dunce of the boomer's camp, "a nobody from nowhar," to use Cal Clemmer's words, came rushing along, hatless and with his wild eyes fairly starting from their sockets.

"Save me! a ghost!" he yelled, swinging his hands over his head. "A ghost full of blood! Oh, oh! I'm a dead boy! I know I am! Stop him from following me!"

"Pumpkin!" ejaculated Dick, striding up and catching the fleeing lad by the arm. "Hold on; what's this racket about?"

The dunce paused, then stood stock still, his mouth opening to its widest extent. He was far from bright, and it took him several seconds to put into words what was passing in his mind.

"About, about?" he repeated. "Dick Arbuckle! Oh, dear me! I've seen your father's ghost!"

"Pumpkin!"

"Yes, I did. Hope to die if I didn't. I was just coming to camp from town. Some men kept me, and made me sing and dance for them--you know how I can sing--tra-la-la-da-do-da-bum! They promised me a dollar, but didn't give it to me. I was running to get out of the wet when I plumped into something fearful--a ghost! Your father, covered with blood, and groaning and moaning, 'Robbed, robbed; almost murdered!' That's what the ghost said, and he caught me by the hand. See, the blood is there yet, even though I did try to wash it off in the rain. Oh, Dick, what does it mean?"

"It means something awful has happened, Pumpkin, if your story is true----"

"Hope to die if it ain't," and the dunce crossed his heart several times. Suddenly, to keep up his courage, he burst into a wild snatch of song:

"A big baboon
Glared at the moon,
And sang la-la-la-dum!
'Come down to me
And I will be
Your lardy-dardy----'"

"Stop it, Pumpkin," interrupted Dick. "Come along with me."

"To where?"

"To where you saw my father."

"Not for a million dollars--not for a million million!" cried the half-witted boy. "It wasn't your father; it was a ghost, all covered with blood!" and he shrank back under the Delaney wagon.

"It was my father, Pumpkin; I am sure of it. He is missing, and something has happened to him. Perhaps he fell and hurt himself. Come on."

The dunce stopped short and stared.

"Missing, is he? Then it wasn't a ghost. La-la-dum! What a joke. Will you go along, too?"

"Of course."

"And take a pistol?"

"Yes."

"Poor mon, Oi thrust he is not very much hurted," broke in Rosy Delaney, who had been a close listener to the foregoing. "If he is, Dick Arbuckle, bring him here, an' it's Rosy Delaney will nurse him wid th' best of care."

As has been said, many had heard Pumpkin Bill's wild cries, but now that he had quieted down these boomers returned to their couches, grumbling that the half-witted lad should thus be allowed to disturb their rest.

In a minute Dick Arbuckle and Pumpkin were hurrying along the road the dunce had previously traveled. The rain was letting up a bit, and the smoky lantern lit up the surroundings for a circle thirty feet in diameter.

"Here is where I met him," said Pumpkin, coming to a halt near the edge of a small stream. "There's the hat he knocked off my head." He picked it up. "Oh, dear me! covered with blood! Did you ever see the like?"

Dick was more disturbed than ever.

"Which way did he go?"

"I don't know."

"Didn't you notice at all, Pumpkin? Try to think."

"Nary a notice. I ran, that's all. It looked like a bloody ghost. I'll dream about it, I know I will."

To this Dick did not answer. Getting down on his knees in the wet he examined the trail by the lantern's rays. The footsteps which he thought must be those of his father led around a bend in the stream and up a series of rocks covered with moss and dirt. With his heart thumping violently under his jacket he followed the footprints until the very summit of the rocks was gained. Then he let out a groan of anguish.

And not without cause. Beyond the summit was a dark opening fifteen feet wide, a hundred or more feet long and of unfathomable depth. The footprints ended at the very edge of this yawning abyss.

CHAPTER II.
DICK ON A RUNAWAY.

I f he fell down here he is dead beyond all doubt!"

Such were Dick Arbuckle's words as he tried in vain to pierce the gloom of the abyss by flashing around the smoky lantern.

"Gosh! I reckon you're right," answered Pumpkin in an awe-struck whisper. "It must be a thousand feet to the bottom of that hole!"

"If I had a rope I might lower myself," went on the youth, with quiet determination. "But without a rope----"

A pounding of hoof-strokes on the grassy trail below the rocks caused him to stop and listen attentively.

"Somebody is coming. I'll see if I can get help!" he cried, and ran down to the trail, swinging his lantern over his head as he went. In ten seconds a horseman burst into view, riding a beautiful racing steed. The newcomer was a well-known leader of the land boomers, who rejoiced in the name of Pawnee Brown.

"Ai! Pawnee Brown!" cried Dick, and at once the leader of the land boomers came to a halt.

"What is it, Arbuckle?" he asked kindly.

"My father is missing, and I have every reason to fear that he has tumbled into an opening at the summit of yonder rocks."

"That's bad, lad. Missing? Since when?"

Dick's story was soon told, and Pawnee Brown at once agreed to go up to the opening and see if anything could be done. "It's the Devil's Chimney," he explained. "If he went over into it I'm afraid he's a goner."

A lariat hung from the pommel of the scout's saddle, and this he took in hand as he dismounted. Soon he stood by the edge of the black opening, while Dick again waved the lantern.

"You and the dunce can lower me by the lariat. I don't believe the opening is more than fifty feet deep," said Pawnee Brown.

The lariat was quickly adjusted around the edge of a smooth rock, and with his foot in a noose and the lantern in hand, the scout was lowered into the depths of the opening.

Down and down he went, the light finding nothing but bare, rocky wall to fall upon. Presently the lowering process ceased.

"We have reached the end of the lariat," called out Dick.

Hardly had he spoken when a fearful thing happened. There was a snap and a whirr, and Dick and Pumpkin went flat on their backs, while ten feet of the lariat whirled loosely over their heads.

The improvised rope had broken.

"Gone!" gasped Dick. "Merciful heavens!"

He scrambled up and looked over the edge of the opening. The lantern had been dashed into a thousand pieces, and all was dark below.

"Pawnee Brown!" he cried, and Pumpkin joined in with a cry which was fairly a shriek.

The opening remained as silent as a tomb. Again and again both called out. Then Dick turned to his companion.

"This is awful, Pumpkin. Something must be done. I shall mount his mare and ride back to camp and get help. For all I know to the contrary both my father and Pawnee Brown are lying dead below."

"I shan't stay here alone," shivered the half-witted boy. Then, before Dick could stop him, he set off at the top of his speed, yelling discordantly as he went.

"Poor fool, he might have ridden with me," thought Dick.

He was already rushing down to the trail. Now he remembered that he had heard a strange noise down where Pawnee Brown's beautiful mare, Bonnie Bird, had been tethered--a noise reaching him just before the lariat had parted. What could that mean?

He reached the clump of trees where Bonnie Bird should have been. The mare was gone!

"Broken away!" he groaned. "Was ever such luck before! Everything is going wrong tonight! Poor father; poor Pawnee Brown! I must leg it to camp just as Pumpkin is doing. Hullo!"

He had started to run, but now he pulled up short. Grazing in the wet grass not a dozen steps away was a bay horse, full and round, a perfect beast. At first Dick Arbuckle thought he must be dreaming. He ran up rubbing his eyes. No, it was no dream; the horse was as real as a horse could be. He was bridled, but instead of a saddle wore only a patch of a blanket.

"It's a Godsend," he murmured. "I don't know whom you belong to, old boy, but you've got to carry me back to camp, and that, too, at a licking gait, you understand?"

The horse pricked up his ears and gave a snort. In a trice Dick was on his back and urging him around in the proper direction. He was a New York boy, not much used to riding, and the management of such a beast as this one did not come easy. The horse arose upon his forelegs and nearly pitched Dick over his head, and the youth had to cling fast around his neck to save himself a lot of broken bones.

"Whoa, there! Gee Christopher, what a tartar! Whoa, I say! If only I had a whip!" he panted, as the horse began to move around on a pivot. "Now, why can't you act nice, when I'm in such dire need of your services? If you don't stop--Whoa! whoa!"

For the horse had suddenly stopped pivoting and started off like a streak, not up or down the trail, but across a stretch of prairie grass. On and on he went, the bit between his teeth and gaining speed at every step. In vain Dick yelled at him, kicked him and banged him on the head. It was of no use, and he had to cling on for dear life.

"I might as well let him go and jump for it," he thought at last, when nearly a mile had been covered. "It's just as useless to try to stop him as it would be to stop a limited express. If I jump off--but I won't, now!"

For the prairie had been left behind, and the bay was tearing along a rocky trail leading to goodness knew where, so Dick thought. A jump now would mean broken bones, perhaps death. He clung tighter than ever, and tried to calm the horse by speaking gently to him.

At first the beast would not listen, but finally, when several miles had been covered he slackened up, and at last dropped into a walk. He was covered with foam, and now he was quite willing to be led.

"You old reprobate!" muttered Dick, as he tightened his hold on the reins. "Now where in the name of creation have you brought me to, and how am I to find my way back to camp from here?"

Sitting upright once again, the youth tried to pierce the darkness. The rain had stopped, only a few scattering drops falling upon himself and the steaming animal, but the darkness was as great as ever.

On two sides of him were forest lands, on the third a slope of rocks and on the fourth a stretch of dwarf grass. The trail, if such it could be called, ran along the edge of the timber. Should he follow this? He moved along slowly, wondering whether he was right or wrong.

"Halt! Who goes there?"

It was a military challenge, coming out of the darkness. Dick stopped the horse, and presently made out the form of a man on horseback, a cavalryman.

"I'm a friend who has lost the way," began the youth, when the cavalryman let out a cry of surprise.

"Tucker's horse, hang me if it isn't! Boy, where did you get that nag? Tucker, Ross, come here! I've collared one of the horse-thieves!"

In a moment more there came the clatter of horses' hoofs through the timber, and Dick found himself surrounded by three big and decidedly ugly-looking United States cavalrymen--troopers who belonged to a detachment set to guard the Oklahoma territory from invasion.

"A boy and a boomer!" ejaculated the fellow named Tucker. "I saw the kid over near Arkansas City a couple of days ago. And riding Chester, too! Git off that hoss, before I kick you off!"

And riding up he caught Dick by the collar and yanked him to the ground. In an instant he was beside the boy and had produced a pair of reservation handcuffs.

"Out with your hands, sonny, and be quick about it."

"What for?" asked Dick, somewhat bewildered by the unceremonious way in which he was being handled. "I didn't steal that horse."

"Too thin, sonny. All you boomers are a set of thieves, and I suppose you think stealing our hossflesh is the rarest kind of a joke. Out with those hands, I say, and consider yourself a prisoner of Uncle Sam. You've nearly ridden Chester to death and for two pins I'd take the law into my own hands and string you up to the nearest tree. Take that!"

And having handcuffed Dick the cavalryman let out with his heavy right hand and landed a savage slap that sent the helpless youth headlong at his feet.

The blow aroused all of the lion in the youth's makeup. As quickly as he could he leaped up.

"You brute!" he cried. "Why don't you fight fair? Take that, and that and that!"

Each "that" meant two blows, for Dick could not separate his hands, and therefore struck out with both at a time--two in the chest, two on the chin and the final pair on either side of Tucker's big and reddish nose. The cavalryman, taken by surprise, let out a cry of rage and pain.

"You imp!" he screamed. "To hit a man in uniform! I'll show you what I can do! How do you like that?"

With incredible swiftness he drew his heavy Sabra and leaped upon Dick. The boy tried to retreat, but slipped on the wet ground and went down. On the instant Tucker was upon him, and, with a fierce cry, the infuriated cavalryman raised his blade over Dick's head.

CHAPTER III.
A CAVE AND A CAVE-IN.

Let us go back and see what happened to Pawnee Brown at the time the lariat parted and he found himself going down into what seemed bottomless space.

Instinctively he put out both hands as far as he was able, to grasp anything which might come within reach and thereby check his awful downward course.

The lantern fell from his fingers and jingled to pieces on a protruding rock.

Then his right hand slid over the ends of a bush growing out of a fissure. He caught the bush and held on like grim death.

The bush gave way, but not instantly, and his descent was checked so that the tumble to the bottom of the hole, fifteen feet further down, was not near as bad as it would otherwise have been.

Yet he came down sideways, and his head striking a flat rock, he was knocked insensible.

Half an hour went by, and he opened his eyes in a wondering way. Where was he and what had happened?

Soon the truth burst upon him, and he staggered to his feet to see if any bones had been broken.

"All whole yet, thanks to my usual good luck," he thought. "But that's a nasty lump on the back of my head. Hullo, up there!"

He called out as loudly as he could, but no answer came back, for Dick and Pumpkin were already gone.

"Well, I always allowed that I would explore the Devil's Chimney some day, but I didn't calculate to do it quite so soon," he went on. "What can have become of those boys? Have they deserted me or gone off for help? If I can read character I fancy that Dick Arbuckle will do all he can for me--and, by the way, can his father's corpse really be down here?"

He brought forth a match and lit it. The battered lantern lay close at hand, and, although without a glass, it was still better than nothing, and, turned well up, gave forth a torch-like flame which lit up the surroundings for a dozen feet or more. No body was there, nor did he find any for the full distance up and down the dismal hole.

"The boy was mistaken; his father wandered elsewhere," was the boomer's conclusion. "Poor fellow, he was in no mental or physical condition to push his claims in the West. He should have remained at home and allowed some hustling Western lawyer to act for him. If he falls into the clutches of some of our land agents they'll swindle him out of every cent of his fortune. I must give him and the boy the tip when I get the chance." The great scout laughed softly. "When I get the chance is good. I reckon I had best pull myself out of this man-trap first."

He made a careful investigation of the rocks. At no point was there anything which gave promise of a footing to the top.

"In a pocket and no error," he mused. "I wonder if I've got to stay here like a bull-croaker at the bottom of a well?"

The rain had formed a long pool between the slanting rocks. He threw a chip into this pool and saw that it drifted slowly off between two scrub bushes growing partly under a shelving rock.

With the light he made an inspection of the locality, and a cry of surprise escaped him. Beyond the bushes was the opening to an irregular, but apparently large cavern.

The stream flowed along one side of the flooring to this opening.

"Must be some sort of an outlet beyond," he mused. "I'll try it and see," and in a moment more he was inside of the cavern and crawling along on hands and knees.

He had not far to go in this fashion. Twenty feet beyond the cavern became so large that he could stand up with ease. He flashed the light above his head.

"By Jove! a miniature Mammoth Cave of Kentucky!" burst from his lips.

On he went until a bend in the formation of the cavern was gained. Here the stream of water disappeared under a pile of loose stones, and the opening became less than six feet in height.

"Checked!" he muttered, and his face fell. It looked as if he would have to go back the way he had come.

Again he raised his light and gazed about him with more care than ever.

The loose rocks soon caught his attention, and, setting down the lantern, he began to pull away first at one and then another.

The last turned back, he saw another opening, evidently leading upward.

"This must lead to the open air--" he began, when a grinding of stone caught his ears. In a twinkle a veritable shower of rocks came down around his head. He was knocked flat and almost covered.

For fully ten minutes he lay gasping for breath. The blood was flowing from a wound on his cheek, and it was a wonder that he had not been killed.

"In the future I'll have more care," he groaned, as, throwing first one stone and then another aside, he sat up. The falling of the stones had been followed by some dirt, and now a regular landslide came after, burying him up to the armpits.

"Planted," was the single word which issued from his lips. He was not seriously hurt, and was half inclined to laugh at his predicament. Still, on the whole, it was no laughing matter, and Pawnee Brown lost no time in trying to dig himself free.

The stones and dirt were wedged tightly about his legs, and not wishing to run the risk of a broken or twisted ankle, the scout worked with care, all the time wondering if Dick Arbuckle was back, and never once dreaming of the peril the poor lad was encountering. The rain was soaking through the ceiling of the cavern, and the situation was far from a comfortable one.

At last he was free again, and striking a match, he hunted up the lantern and lit it once more.

The opening to the inner cave was now large enough to pass through with ease, and making sure of his footing, the scout moved forward, straining his eyes eagerly for some sign of an egress to the outer world.

Presently he saw a number of straggly things dangling downward from the rocks and soil overhead.

They were the bottom roots of some great tree standing fifteen or twenty feet above.

"Not far from the surface now, that's certain," he thought, with considerable satisfaction. "And yet, hang me if I can see an opening of any sort yet."

On and on he went, until nearly a hundred feet more had been passed.

The cave had widened out, but now it narrowed once again to less than a dozen feet. The roof, too, sloped downward until it occasionally scraped the crown of his sombrero.

The light of the lantern began to splutter and flare up, showing that the oil in the cup was running low.

"If only the thing lasts until I find the door to this confounded prison," he thought.

Suddenly a peculiar hiss sounded out upon the darkness.

Pawnee Brown knew that hiss only too well, and leaping back he snatched a pistol from his belt.

The hiss was followed by a rattle, and now, flashing the light around, the scout saw upon a flat rock the curled-up form of a huge rattlesnake.

The eyes of the reptile shone like twin stars, and when Pawnee Brown discovered him he was getting ready to strike.

The rattler was less than six feet away, and the scout knew that he could cover that space with ease. Therefore, whatever was to be done must be done quickly.

Like a flash the pistol came up. But ere Pawnee Brown could fire a curious thing happened.

A large drop of water, splashing down from the roof of the cavern, caused the light to splutter and go out.

The scout was in the dark with his enemy.

More than this, he was boxed up in a narrow place, from which escape was well-nigh impossible.

Aiming as best he could under the circumstances, he fired.

The bullet struck the flat rock, bounded up to the side wall of the cavern and then hit him in the leg.

"Missed, by thunder!"

He jumped past the spot and moved up the cavern a distance of several yards.

A rattle and a whirr followed, as the great rattlesnake made a vicious strike in the dark. An intense hiss sounded out when the reptile realized that the object of his anger had been missed.

Listening with strained ears, the boomer heard the deadly thing sliding slowly from rock to rock, coming closer at every movement.

To flee was impossible, so with bated breath he stood his ground.

CHAPTER IV.
OUT OF THE CAVERN.

Slowly but surely the great rattlesnake came closer to where Pawnee Brown stood motionless in the darkness of the cavern.

The reptile had been enraged by the shot the great scout fired, and now meant to strike, and that fatally.

Listening with ears strained to their utmost, the boomer heard the form of the snake slide from rock to rock of the uneven flooring.

The rattler was all of ten feet long and as thick around as a good-sized fence rail.

One square strike from those poisonous fangs and Pawnee Brown's hours would be numbered.

Yet the scout did not intend to give up his life just now. He still held his pistol, four chambers of which were loaded.

"If only I had a light," he thought.

Retreat was out of the question. A single sound and the rattlesnake would have been upon him like a flash.

It was only the darkness and the utter silence that made the reptile cautious.

Suddenly the scout heard a scraping on the rocks less than three feet in front of him.

The time for action had come; another moment and the rattler would be wound around his legs.

Crack! crack! Two reports rang out in quick succession and by the flash of the first shot Pawnee Brown located those glittering eyes.

The second shot went true to its mark, and the rattler dropped back with a hole through its ugly head.

The long, whip like body slashed hither and thither, and the scout had to do some lively sprinting to keep from getting a tangle and a squeeze.

As he hopped about he struck a match, picked up the lantern, shook the little oil remaining into the wick and lit it. Another shot finished the snake and the body curled up into a snarl and a quiver, to bother him no more.

It was then that Pawnee Brown paused, drew a deep breath and wiped the cold perspiration from his brow.

"By gosh! I've killed fifty rattlers in my time, but never one in this fashion," he murmured. "Wonder if there are any more around?"

He knew that these snakes often travel in pairs, and as he went on his way he kept his eyes wide open for another attack.

But none came, and now something else claimed his attention.

The cavern was coming to an end. The side walls closed in to less than three feet, and the flooring sloped up so that he had to crouch down and finally go forward on his hands and knees.

The lantern now went out for good, every drop of oil being exhausted.

At this juncture many a man would have halted and turned back to where he had come from, but such was not Pawnee Brown's intention.

"I'll see the thing through," he muttered. "I'd like to know how far I am from the surface of the ground."

A dozen yards further and the cavern become so small that additional progress was impossible.

He placed his hand above him and encountered nothing but dirt, with here and there a small stone.

With care he began to dig away at the dirt with his knife. Less than a foot of the cavern ceiling had thus been dug away when the point of the knife brought down a small stream of water.

Feeling certain he was now close to the surface, he continued to work with renewed vigor.

"At last!"

The scout was right. The knife had found the outer air, and a dim, uncertain light struck down upon the hero of the plains.

It did not take long to enlarge the opening sufficiently to admit the passage of

Pawnee Brown's body.

He leaped out among a number of bushes and stretched himself.

Having brushed the dirt from his wet clothing, he "located himself," as he put it, and started up a hill to the entrance to the Devil's Chimney.

He was on the side opposite to that from which he had descended, and, in order to get over, had to make a wide detour through some brush and small timber.

This accomplished, he hurried to where he had left Bonnie Bird tethered.

As the reader knows, the beautiful mare was gone, and had been for some time.

"I suppose that young Arbuckle took her," he mused. "But, if so, why doesn't he come back here with her?"

There being no help for it, the scout set off for the camp of the boomers on foot.

He was just entering the temporary settlement when he came face to face with Jack Rasco, another of the boomers.

"Pawnee!" shouted the boomer, "You air jess the man I want ter see. Hev ye sot eyes on airy o' the Arbuckles?"

"I'm looking for Dick Arbuckle now," answered the scout. "Isn't he in the camp? I thought he came here with my mare?"

"He ain't nowhar. Rosy Delaney says he went off with Pumpkin to look for his dad, who had disappeared----"

"Then he didn't come back? What can have become of him and Bonnie Bird?" Pawnee Brown's face grew full of concern. "Something is wrong around here, Jack," he continued, and told the boomer of what had happened up at the Devil's Chimney. "First it's the father, and now it's the son and my mare. I must investigate this."

"I'm with yer, Pawnee--with yer to the end. Yer know thet."

"Yes, Jack; you are one of the few men I know I can trust in everything. But two of us are not enough. If harm has befallen the Arbuckles it is the duty of the whole camp--or, at least, every man in it--to try to sift matters to the bottom."

"Right ye air, Pawnee. I'll raise a hullabaloo and rouse 'em up."

Jack Rasco was as good as his word. Going from wagon to wagon, he shook the sleepers and explained matters. In less than a quarter of an hour a dozen stalwart boomers were in the saddle, while Jack Rasco brought forth an extra horse of his own for Brown's use.

"Has anybody seen the dunce?" questioned the scout.

No one had since he had gone off with Dick to look for the so-called ghost.

"We will divide up into parties of two," said Pawnee Brown, and this was done, and soon he and Jack Rasco were bounding over the trail leading toward the Indian Territory, while others were setting off in the direction of Arkansas City and elsewhere.

"Something curious about them air Arbuckles," observed Rasco as they flew along side by side. "Mortimer Arbuckle said as how he was coming hyer fer his health, but kick me ef I kin see it."

"I think myself the man has an axe to grind," responded the leader of the boomers. "You know he came West to see about some land."

"Oh, I know thet. But thar's somethin' else, sure ez shootin' ez shootin', Pawnee. It kinder runs in my noddle thet he is a'lookin' fer somebuddy."

"Who?"

"Ah, thar's where ye hev got me. But I'll tell ye something. One night when the boy wuz over ter Arkansas City the old man war sleeping in the wagon, an' he got a nightmare. He clenched his fists an' begun ter moan an' groan. 'Don't say I did it, Bolange,' he moans. 'Don't say that--it's an awful crime! Don't put the blood on my head!' an' a lot more like thet, till my blood most run cold an' I shook him ter make him wake up. Now, don't thet look like he had something on his mind?"

"It certainly does, and yet the man is not quite right in his upper story, although I wouldn't tell the son that, Rasco. But what was the name he mentioned?"

"Bolange, or Volange, or something like thet. It seems ter me he hollered out Louis onct, too."

A sudden light shone in the great scout's eyes. He gripped his companion by the arm.

"Try to think, Jack. Did Arbuckle speak the name of Vorlange--Louis Vorlange?"

"By gosh! Pawnee, you hev struck it--Vorlange, ez plain ez day. Do yer know the man?"

"Do I know him?" Pawnee Brown drew a long breath. "Jack, I believe I once told you about my schoolboy days at Wellington and elsewhere before I left home to take up a life on the cattle trails?"

"Yes, Pawnee. From all accounts you wuz cut out for a schoolmaster, instead of a leader of us boomers."

"I was a professor once at the Indian Industrial school at Pawnee Agency. That is where I got to be called Pawnee Brown, and where the Pawnees became so friendly that they made me their white chief. But I aspired to something more than teaching and more than cow punching in those boyhood days at Wellington; I wanted to have a try at entrance to West Point and follow in the footsteps of Grant and Custer, and fellows of that sort."

"Ye deserved it, I'll bet, Pawnee."

"I worked hard for it, and at last I got a chance to compete at the examination. Among the other boys who competed was Louis Vorlange. He had been the bully of our school, and more than once we had fought, and twice I had sent him to bed with a head that was nearly broken. He hated me accordingly, and swore I should not win the prize I coveted."

"Did he try, too?"

"Yes, but he was outclassed from the start, for, although he was sly and shrewd, book learning was too much for him. The examination came off, and I got left, through Vorlange, who stole my papers and changed many of my answers. I didn't learn of this until it was too late. My chance of going to West Point fell through. There was nothing to do but to thrash Vorlange, and the day before I left home I gave him a licking that I'll wager he'll remember to the day of his death. As it was, he tried to shoot me, but I collared the pistol, and for that dastardly attack knocked two of his teeth down his throat."

"Served him right, Pawnee. But I don't see whar--"

"Hold on a minute, Jack. I said Vorlange didn't go to West Point; but he was strong with the politicians, and as soon as he was old enough he got a position under the government, and now I understand he is somewhere around the Indian Territory acting as a spy for the land department."

"By gosh! I see. An' ye think Mortimer Arbuckle knows this same chap?"

"It would look so. If I can read faces, the old man is innocent of wrong-doing, and if that is so and there is the secret of a crime between him and Louis Vorlange you can wager Vorlange is the guilty party."

"Pawnee, you hev a head on yer shoulders fit fer a judge, hang me ef ye ain't," burst out Jack Rasco admiringly. "I wish yer would talk to Arbuckle the next time he turns up. Mebbe yer kin lift a weight off o' his shoulders. The poor old fellow-- creation! wot's that?"

Jack Rasco stopped short and pulled up his horse. A wild, unearthly scream rent the air, rising and falling on the wind of the night. The scream was followed by a burst of laughter which was truly demoniacal.

Pawnee Brown pulled his horse up on his haunches. What was this new mystery which confronted him?

Again the cry rang out; but now the scout recognized it and a faint smile shone upon his face.

"It's the dunce," he exclaimed. "Pumpkin! Pumpkin! Come here!"

A moment of silence followed and he called again. Then from the brush which grew among the rocks emerged the form of the half-witted boy.

"Pumpkin, where is Dick Arbuckle?" questioned Pawnee Brown, leaping to the ground and catching the lad by his arm.

"Lemme go! I didn't hurt him!" screamed Pumpkin. "He went that way--like the wind--on a bay horse which was running away. Oh, he's killed, I know he is!"

"You are sure of this?"

"Hope to die if it ain't so. Poor Dick! He'll be pitched off and smashed up like his father was smashed up. Hurry, and maybe you can catch him."

"I believe the dunce speaks the truth," broke in Jack Rasco.

"How long ago was this?"

"Not more'n an hour. Hurry up if you want to save him," and with a yell such as he had uttered before, Pumpkin disappeared.

Pawnee Brown and Rasco wasted no more time. Whipping up their steeds, they set off on a rapid gallop in the direction the runaway horse had pursued.

CHAPTER V.
THE CAVALRYMEN.

Let us rejoin Dick Arbuckle at the time that the incensed cavalryman, Tucker, was about to attack the hapless lad with his heavy Sabra.

Had the cruel blow fallen as intended it is beyond dispute that Dick would have been severely injured.

"Don't!" cried the boy, and then closed his eyes at the terrible thought of such dire punishment so close at hand.

But just at that instant an interruption came from out of the darkness of the brush.

"Hello, there! What are you up to?"

Tucker started, and the Sabra was turned aside to bury itself in the exposed roots of a tree.

"If it ain't Pawnee Brown!" muttered another cavalryman, Ross by name.

"Pawnee Brown!" burst from Dick's lips, joyfully, and, rising, he attempted to rush toward his friend.

"Not so fast, boy!" howled Tucker, and caught the youth by the collar.

"What's the meaning of this? What are you doing to that boy?" asked Pawnee Brown as he rode closer, with Rasco beside him.

"He's a horse thief, and we are going to take him to our camp," answered Tucker, somewhat uneasily, for he had seen Pawnee Brown before and knew he had a man of strong character with whom to deal.

"A horse thief!" ejaculated Jack Rasco. "Say, sod'ger, yer crazy! Thet boy a thief! Wall, by gum!"

"That boy is no thief," put in Pawnee Brown. "He belongs to our camp, and is as square as they make them--I'll vouch for it."

"I ain't taking the word of any boomer," muttered Tucker sourly. "That kid--hold on! Don't shoot!"

And he dropped back in terror, for the great scout had drawn his pistol like a flash.

"You'll take my word or take something else," came the stiff response. "Be quick, now, and say which you choose."

"I didn't mean any harm, Pawnee. Maybe you don't know it, but the boy is a thief just the same. We just caught him riding my horse--this bay. My comrades can prove it."

"It's true," said Ross.

"True as gospel," added Skimmy, the third cavalryman. "We caught him less than half an hour ago."

Without answering to this, Pawnee Brown turned to the youth.

"Tell me your yarn, Dick. I know there is some mistake here."

"There is not much to tell, Major. When the lariat broke up at the Devil's Chimney and I couldn't make you reply to my calls I ran off to get help and a rope. I intended to ride your mare back to camp, but when I got to where the mare had been tethered I found her gone and this bay loafing around in her place. I got on the bay, but, instead of riding to camp, the animal ran away with me and brought me here. These fellows were mighty rough on me, and that man was going to split my head open when you came along in the nick of time."

"That's a neat fairy tale," sneered Tucker. "This horse was stolen four hours ago. More than likely the boy couldn't manage him and lost his way and the horse tried to get back to where he belonged."

"That doesn't connect with what I know," answered Pawnee Brown, quietly. "My mare was tethered where he went to look for her. I might as well accuse you of riding down there, taking Bonnie Bird and leaving this nag in her place."

"Do you mean to insinuate we are horse thieves?" cried Ross hotly.

"I'm giving you as good as you send, that's all. Dick, have you any idea where Bonnie Bird is?"

"Not the slightest, sir."

The great scout heaved a sigh. The little racing mare was the very apple of his eye.

"I'll not give up the hunt until I have found her." He turned again to the caval-rymen. "If the finest little black mare, with a white blaze, that you ever saw strays into your camp remember she belongs to me," he went on. "I want her returned at once, and if anybody attempts to keep her there will be a hotter time than this Territory has seen for many a day. Dick, hop up behind me," and he turned to his horse.

"That boy is to remain here," blustered Tucker, growing red in the face.

"Hardly, my bantam. Hop up, Dick, and we'll strike back for camp before the sun comes up and see if the others who are on the search have seen anything of your father. I saw nothing of him at the bottom of the Devil's Chimney."

"I'm not going to have a lazy, good-for-nothing boomer lay it over me----" be-gan Tucker, when once more the sight of Pawnee Brown's pistol silenced him.

No more was said as the scout, Dick and Rasco rode away down the trail by which they had come. But, once out of sight, Tucker raised his fist and shook it savagely.

"I'll get square with you some day, Pawnee Brown, mark my words!" he mut-tered between his set teeth.

"We'll all get square," said Ross. "I hate the sight of that man."

"I understand the boomers have made him their leader," broke in Skimmy. "If they have, he'll try to break through to Oklahoma as sure as guns are guns."

"And he'll get shot, too," answered Tucker dryly. "The lieutenant is having all of the boomers' movements watched."

"Pawnee Brown will do his level best to give us the slip, see if he don't," re-marked Skimmy. "Four thousand boomers wouldn't make him their leader for nothing."

Thus, talking among themselves, the three cavalrymen mounted their horses and rode back to their various picket stations along the boundary line of the Indian Territory.

They were a detachment of the Seventh United States Cavalry, and the lieuten-ant referred to by Tucker was in command.

For over a month they had been watching the boomers assembling in Kansas. Other portions of the United States troops were watching the would-be Oklahoma settlers in Arkansas and Texas.

There was every prospect of a lively time ahead, and it was not far off.

Reaching his station, Tucker drew from his pocket a briar-root pipe, filled and lit it and began to puff away meditatively.

His face had been ugly before, but now as he began to meditate it grew blacker than ever.

"Hang me, if everything ain't going wrong," he muttered. "I won't stand it. I'll make a kick, and when I do----" He paused as a shadow among the trees caught his eye. "Who goes there?" he called out and drew his pistol.

"A friend. Tucker, is that you?"

"Vorlange!" cried the cavalryman, and the next moment the newcomer and the military man were face to face.

"It's about time you showed up," growled Tucker, after a brief pause, during which the newcomer looked at him anxiously. "Say, Vorlange, when do you intend to settle up with me. Give it to me straight, now."

"That's why I left the trail to hunt you up, Tucker--I knew you were anxious about that five hundred dollars."

"Why shouldn't I be? It took me a long time to save it--a good sight longer than it did for you to gamble it away."

"Tucker, I didn't gamble that away--I'll swear it. I used it in business."

"Business? What business have you got outside of your position as a land office spy?"

"A good business, if you only knew it. I've been following up a little deal that started in the East--in New York. Out there I had to hire a fellow I could trust to work for me, and that took most of the money. But the whole thing is coming my way now, and I want to talk things over with you. How would you like to have a thousand back in return for the five hundred you loaned me?"

"What sort of a game are you working on me now?"

"A square deal, Tucker. I've been keeping my eye on you, and I reckon you are the fellow to do what I want done."

"And what do you want done?"

Vorlange stepped closer.

"The boomers are going to try to cross into Oklahoma either to-morrow or day after. There will be a fight, I am certain of it, and somebody will be shot and killed.

When you fire I want you to pick out your man--two men--or, rather, a man and a boy, if you can do it. I may be on hand to take part myself, but there is a possibility that I may be ordered elsewhere."

"And you are willing to pay me five hundred extra for picking out my target, Vorlange?"

"You've struck it."

"Who is the man?"

"Can I trust you?"

"Yes."

"Pawnee Brown."

At the mention of the great scout's name Tucker started back.

"Why--why do you want him knocked over?"

"He is my enemy. I have hated him from my boyhood!" cried Louis Vorlange. "And there are other reasons--he stands in the way of my pushing the scheme I mentioned."

"Pawnee Brown was here but a short while ago. He insulted and abused me," growled Tucker. "I'll put a bullet through him quick enough if I get the chance--that is, in a skirmish. I don't want to run any risk of being strung up for--you know."

"The shooting will be O. K., Tucker, and I'll help if I'm not ordered away. Do it and the five hundred extra are yours, I'll give you my word."

"What about that boy you mentioned?"

"His name is Dick Arbuckle. He is----"

"Dick Arbuckle? I know him. He stole my horse. I captured him and Pawnee Brown came to his rescue and made me, Ross and Skimmy give him up," and Tucker gave the particulars in his own version of the affair.

"Then you bear the lad no love?"

"Love?" The cavalryman grated his teeth. "I was wishing I could get a shot at him."

"Then keep that wish in mind, Tucker, when the time for action arrives."

"If it's worth five hundred to you to have Pawnee Brown knocked over it ought to be worth more to have both of 'em laid low," suggested Tucker, who was naturally a grasping fellow.

"Five hundred in cold cash is a good deal in these times," was the slow answer.

"But I'll tell you what I'll do. If, after a fight, you can bring me absolute proof that Pawnee Brown and Dick Arbuckle are dead I'll give you an even twelve hundred dollars, the five hundred I borrowed and seven hundred extra. There's my hand on it. What do you say?"

"Will you promise to give me the money as soon as you have the proofs?"

"I will," and Louis Vorlange raised his right hand as though to make good such a blasphemous promise.

"All right, then; I take you up," answered Tucker.

CHAPTER VI.
DICK'S HUNT.

D on't you take it so hard, my lad; I feel certain that your father will turn up sooner or later."

It was Pawnee Brown who spoke. He addressed Dick, who sat on a horse belonging to Jack Rasco. The pair had been scouring the plains and the woods for three hours in search of Dick's father.

"Poor father! If only I knew what had become of him!" sighed the lad.

In his anxiety he had forgotten all about his adventures among the cavalrymen who had sought to detain him as a horse thief.

"It's a mystery, thet's what it is," burst in Jack Rasco.

"It looks loike the hivens hed opened an' swalleyed him up," was Mike Delaney's comment. "Be jabbers, we all know th' hivens was wide open enough last noight. Me turn-out is afther standin' in two foot o' wather, an' Rosy raisin' the mischief because she can't go out. 'Moike,' sez she, 'Moike Delaney, git a boat or Oi'll be drowned,' an' niver a boat in sight. Th' ould woman will have to shtay in the wagon till the wather runs off of itself."

"I wonder if it is possible my poor father wandered into town," mused Dick. "Perhaps he did that and was locked up by the police. He is--well, you know he gets strange spells," and the youth's face flushed.

"Run into town, lad, and make a search," answered the boomer. "If I and Rasco get the chance we'll follow. We shan't strike camp for several hours yet."

Dick thought this good advice and was soon on his way. The rain had stopped entirely and the sun was just peeping up over the distant plains when he entered Arkansas City and began his hunt.

A visit to the police station speedily revealed the fact that nothing was known there concerning his missing parent. Here Dick left a description of his father, and was promised that if anything was discovered of the man word would be sent to him immediately.

Having ridden around to the depot, hotels and other public places, Dick tied up his steed and began a hunt through the various streets, looking into the doors of the stores and saloons as he passed.

His footsteps soon brought him down to the vicinity of the river front. Here, situated along several blocks, were a number of eating and drinking houses, patronized principally by river men, gamblers and similar persons.

Having satisfied himself, with a sigh of relief, that his father was not in any of the saloons, the youth came to a halt in front of a restaurant. He had not eaten anything since the evening before, and his night of adventures had made him decidedly hungry.

"I'll get a cup of coffee and some rolls to brace me up," he thought, and entered the establishment. His order was soon given, and he took a seat at a side table, close to a thin board partition.

His order served, he was disposing of the last of it, when the sound of voices on the other side of the partition attracted his attention.

"Leave me alone, Juan Donomez!" came in the voice of a girl. "You have no right to touch me."

"You are too pretty to be left alone," came in the slick tones of a Mexican vaquero. "Come, now, senorita, give me just one kiss."

"I will not, and you must leave me alone," went on the girl, and her trembling voice showed plainly that she was much frightened. "Where is the man who sent for me?"

"He is not here yet."

"I do not believe he sent for me at all. It was a trick of yours to get me here. Let me go."

"Not yet, senorita; you can go after a while. But first you must give me a kiss. Then I will explain why I had you come."

As the last words were uttered Dick heard a scurry of feet, then came a faint scream, cut short by the Mexican. The boy waited to hear no more.

"The contemptible greaser!" he muttered and leaped up. Throwing down the amount of his check on the cashier's desk he hurried from the restaurant. As he had supposed there was a hallway next door, where the talking he had overheard was taking place.

"Oh, save me!" cried the girl, and one glance at her told Dick that she was not over sixteen and as beautiful as any maiden he had ever seen. She was attired in true western style and wore on her mass of shining curls a big, soft riding hat.

"Let that young lady alone," cried the youth to the Mexican, who glared at him savagely. "I overheard your talk, and if she wants to leave she shall do it."

"Oh, thank you for coming to my aid," burst out the girl gratefully. "This bad man----"

"Say no more, Nellie Winthrop," interrupted the Mexican. "Go to the rear. I will attend to this cub who dares to interfere with my business."

And he shoved the girl behind him. His roughness made Dick's blood boil over, and, rushing forward, he put out his foot, gave a push, and Juan Donomez measured his length upon the floor.

During the encounter Nellie Winthrop had escaped to the front end of the hallway, and here Dick now joined her.

"We might as well go," said the youth.

"Yes, yes; let us get out as quickly as we can," answered the girl trembling. "He may attempt to attack you."

"I ought to hand him over to the authorities, but I won't," said Dick. "Come," and he opened the door and followed her to the street.

"I shall never forget you for your kindness," the girl burst out as soon as they had left the vicinity of the spot where the trouble had occurred. "You are very brave, Mr.----"

"I'm only Dick Arbuckle, Miss----"

"Nellie Winthrop is my name. I just reached Arkansas City yesterday. I am from Peoria, and am looking for my uncle, who is somewhere among the Oklahoma boomers."

"Indeed! I'm one of the boomers myself--at least, I've been with them a good part of the time. Perhaps I know your uncle. What is his name?"

"John Rasco, but I believe the men all call him Jack Rasco."

"Why, is it possible! I know Jack Rasco well--in fact, my father and I have been stopping with him ever since we came on from New York. As soon as the rush into Oklahoma was over my father was going to get your uncle to locate a certain mine claim in the West for him--a claim that belongs to us, but which can't be located very easily, it seems."

"And where is my uncle now?" demanded Nellie Winthrop.

"At the boomers' camp, I suppose. You see," went on Dick, his face falling, "there is something wrong afoot." And in a few words he told of his father's disappearance and of the search being made to find him.

"I sincerely trust he is safe," said Nellie when he had concluded. "I presume you want to resume your search. Do not let me detain you. If you are among the boomers we will certainly meet again," and she held out her hand.

"Do you feel safe enough to find the camp alone?" he asked. "Perhaps I had better take you there. It is about a mile in that direction," and he indicated the locality with a wave of his hand.

"I feel safe enough in the open air," she smiled. "It was only when that Mexican had me cornered in a dark hallway that I felt alarmed. I was born and brought up on the plains, and I've been to Peoria only to get educated, as they say. I've a horse at the livery stable, and I can ride the distance."

"May I ask how you fell in with that greaser?"

"I think he overheard me asking for my uncle at the hotel, and after that he sent a note saying my uncle was at the place where you found me. I saw him first on the train, where he tried his best to get some information from me about some horses. But I told him little," concluded the girl.

Five minutes later they parted at the livery stable, where Nellie had left her horse, and Dick went on his way to continue his search for his lost parent. The girl had thanked him again for what he had done and had squeezed his hand so warmly that his heart thumped pretty hard, while his face was flushed more than ever before.

CHAPTER VII.
OUT ON THE RIVER.

For over half an hour longer Dick tramped the streets of the city looking for some trace of his father.

Presently he found himself down by the docks along the muddy river. The stream was much swollen, and the few boats tied up were bumping freely against the shore as the current swung them in.

"I wonder if father could have come down here?" he mused. "He had a great fondness for the water when he got those strange spells."

Slowly and with eyes wide open he moved down the river shore, ready to seize upon any evidence which might present itself.

Suddenly he uttered a cry and leaped down into a rowboat lying before, him.

"Father's hat! I'd know it among a thousand!"

Dick was right. There on the stern seat of the craft rested the head-covering Mortimer Arbuckle had worn ever since he had left New York.

The tears stood in the youth's eyes as he picked up the hat and inspected it. One side of the brim was covered with dirt, and it was still soaked from the rain.

"Poor father! Is it possible he fell overboard?"

Dick said "fell overboard," but he thought something else. He knew as well as anybody that his father did strange things while under the influence of the melancholy spells which at times haunted him.

He looked up and down the stream. Nothing was in sight but the boats and here and there a mass of driftwood.

He sat down on the seat and covered his face with his hands.

"Say, boy, wot yer doin' in my boat?"

It was a burly fellow standing upon the shore who asked the question.

"Excuse me; I am looking for my father, who is missing. I just found his hat on the seat here. Did you see anything of him?"

"Missing, eh--an' thet's his headgear? Say, boy, thet's no laughin' matter," and the burly fellow looked at the youth kindly.

"I know it. I am afraid he tumbled overboard. He had times when he wasn't feeling quite right in his head."

The burly individual whistled softly to himself. "Then I reckon Sary was right, arter all," he half mused.

"Sary? Who do you mean?"

"Sary's my wife. She woke me up about five o'clock this mornin'. We live up in the shanty yonder. Sary said she heard somebody moanin' an' yellin' down here. I said she wuz dreamin', but I allow now ez I might hev been mistook, eh?"

"You didn't come out to investigate?"

"No; it war too stormy. I listened, but there wuz no more of the noise arter Sary waked me up. If yer father fell overboard I'm mighty sorry fer yer. If he did go over his body must be a long way down stream by this time."

"Poor father!" It was all Dick could say. He and his parent had been alone in the wide world, and now to think that his only relative was gone was almost beyond endurance.

"Take the boat and go down if yer want to," went on the burly individual. "Ye can leave the craft at Woolley's mill. I'd go along, only the old woman's took sick an' I've got to hustle fer a doctor."

"I will take a look around in the boat," answered Dick, and, having procured the oars, he set off. The current was so strong it was not necessary to use the blades, and he had all he could do to keep the craft from spinning around and dashing itself against the shore or the other boats which lay along both banks.

On and on the rowboat sped, until about a quarter of a mile had been covered. Nothing unusual had yet been noted, yet the boy kept his eyes strained for some sign of his father, praying inwardly that all might still be well with the only one who was left to him.

"If father is dead, what shall I do?" he thought with a shiver. "He had all of our money with him, all of those precious papers, everything. I would be left a pauper, and, worse than that, without a single relative in the wide world. Oh, pray Heaven he is spared to me!"

"Look out there, youngster!"

It was a wild cry, coming from a bend in the stream. Dick had been gazing across the river. Now he turned to behold his craft rushing swiftly toward the trunk of a half-submerged tree which the storm had torn away from the shore.

The river was almost a torrent at this place.

He grasped the oars, intending to turn the boat from its mad course. But the action came too late. Crash! The craft struck a sharp branch of the tree with fearful force, staving in the bow completely, and the next instant the boy was hurled headlong into the boiling and foaming current.

CHAPTER VIII.
EXPOSING A SWINDLER.

It was less than an hour after separating from Dick Arbuckle that Pawnee Brown found his way to Arkansas City.

He was accompanied by Jack Rasco and Cal Clemmer, and the great scout's object was not alone to aid Dick in the search for Mortimer Arbuckle, but also to help Cal Clemmer get back some money out of which the cowboy boomer claimed he had been swindled.

Clemmer had played cards with a certain sharp known as Pete Stillwater, and lost two hundred and fifty dollars. At first he had imagined he had lost it fairly enough, but after thoughts, coupled with what he heard on the sly the next day, made him certain that Stillwater had cheated him.

He had brought his case to Pawnee Brown, and the leader of the boomers at once concluded that the gambler had not acted fairly. He had met Stillwater at Wichita, where the gambler's reputation was far from savory.

"You were a fool to bet at cards, Cal," he said flatly. "But that is no reason why Stillwater should cheat you. I'll do what I can, but you must promise to leave playing for high stakes alone in the future."

"Don't yer fear, Pawnee," was Clemmer's ready reply. "A scorched Injun keeps hez distance from the blaze, don't he? Wall, I'm the scorched Injun in this air case. Git back my money fer me an' I won't play nothin' higher then penny-ante ez long ez I live."

The gambling resort at which Stillwater was holding forth was soon reached, and the three entered, to find the place comfortably crowded by boomers, men-about-town, cowboys and gamblers, all anxious to add to their wealth without working. As Pawnee Brown surveyed the assemblage his lip curled with a sarcasm which was by no means displaced.

"Poor fools!" he thought; "they expect to win, and nine-tenths of them are bound in the end to be fleeced out of all they possess. Why men who have brains will throw away good money in this fashion is more than I can understand."

"Thar's Stillwater," whispered Cal Clemmer. "Hang hez hide, I'd like ter wring hez neck fer him."

"Better wring his money bag first," smiled Pawnee Brown.

Without hesitation he called Stillwater outside and explained the situation.

"You can say what you please, Stillwater," he said. "I am certain you have been cheating, for I know your past record. You must restore that money and do it right away."

A stormy war of words followed, but Pawnee Brown was firm and at last Stillwater gave up about a hundred dollars--all he had with him.

He went off vowing vengeance and when at a safe distance turned and drew a pistol from his pocket.

"He's going to shoot ye!" cried one of the boomers, but Stillwater was afraid to fire. As Pawnee Brown started after him on a run the gambler fled toward the river.

"Let us go after him!" cried one of the others, and away they went. Soon they came in sight of the river and saw Stillwater in a small craft, sculling his way to the opposite shore. Presently a bend in the stream hid him from view.

"Hullo!" sang out Pawnee Brown. "Here comes another rowboat, and--yes, there is Dick Arbuckle in it. What can he be doing on the river?"

"The boat is makin' fer thet half-sunk tree!" interrupted Cal Clemmer. "He'll strike ef he don't look out! Heavens!"

"Look out there, youngster!" yelled Pawnee Brown, and those were the words which attracted Dick's attention, as mentioned in the former chapter.

It was useless to say more. Standing upon the bank, Pawnee Brown and the cowboy boomer saw the craft strike and go to pieces and saw Dick thrown out into the madly rushing current.

As the boy sped along his head came into painful contact with the furthest of the tree branches, and he was partially stunned. His eyes closed and he struck out wildly and ineffectually.

"He'll be drowned!" gasped Clemmer. "It would take a strong swimmer to gain the bank with the water runnin' ez it is to-day."

"I don't believe he could catch a rope," answered Pawnee Brown, starting off down the river bank. "Cal, hunt one up somewhere; I'm going in after him!"

"But the risk----"

"Never mind the risk. Get the rope if you can," and away went the scout again.

"Help!" came faintly from Dick. He was dazed and weak, and could hardly see in what direction the shore really was.

"Keep up, boy, and we'll save you!" shouted Pawnee Brown encouragingly.

Reaching a spot twenty or thirty feet below where Dick was drifting, he threw off his hat and coat and leaped into the stream.

Down he went over his head, to come up a second later and strike out powerfully for the youth. The cold water chilled him, but to this he paid no attention. He had taken a fancy to Dick, and was resolved to save the boy at any cost.

Nearer and nearer he came. It was a tough struggle, for in the bend of the swollen stream the water boiled and foamed upon all sides. He was yet ten feet away from Dick, when he saw the youth sink beneath the surface.

"Gone!" he thought, and made a leap and a dive. His outstretched hand came in contact with Dick's left arm, and he dragged his burden upward.

"Keep cool, Dick," he said when he could speak. "Can't you swim?"

"Yes, but not extra well," panted the half-drowned lad. "I struck my head upon something."

"Then lay hold of my shoulder and I'll keep you up. Steady, now, or the current will send us around like two tops."

No more was said, as both felt they must save their breath. With Dick clinging loosely, so as not to hinder his swimming, Pawnee Brown struck out for the shore.

It was perilous work, for other trees and obstructions were upon every hand, and more than once both were torn and scratched as they sped by in what was little short of a whirlpool.

"Catch the rope!" suddenly came from Clemmer, and a noose whizzed in the air and fell close beside the pair. Both Pawnee Brown and Dick did as requested, and the cowboy boomer began to haul in with all the strength at his command. It was hard work, but Clemmer was equal to it, and presently those in the water came close enough to gain a footing, and then the peril was over.

Dick's story was soon told, to which the great scout added that of his own.

"I shall not attempt to follow up Stillwater," Pawnee Brown concluded. "It is high time I got back to camp, for let me tell you, privately, we move westward to-day. You may continue the hunt for your father or come with me, just as you choose. It is possible you may find some trace of him around here, but it is doubtful to me, after such a storm. It's hard lines, boy, but cheer up; things may not be as bad as you imagine," and he laid a dripping but affectionate arm upon Dick's shoulder.

"I will stay here for a while, at least," answered Dick. "But--but I am without a cent, and----"

"How much do you want, Dick?" and Pawnee Brown's pocketbook came out without delay.

"If you will lend me ten dollars----"

"Here are twenty. When you want more let me know. Now, goodbye, and good luck to you."

And the next minute Pawnee Brown and Clemmer were gone. Dick watched them out of sight and a warm feeling went over his heart.

"The major is as generous as he is brave," he murmured. "He is one scout of a thousand. No wonder all the boomers asked him to lead them in this expedition."

Ten minutes later Dick was drying himself at the fire in a house near by. Hearing his tale of misfortune, the man who took him in insisted upon treating him to some hot coffee, which did a good bit toward making him feel once more like himself.

"It may be a wild-goose chase, but I can't give it up," he muttered as he continued his search by walking along the river bank. "Poor father, where can he be?"

The outskirts of the city had been left behind and he was making his way through a tangle of brush and over shelving rocks. A bend was passed and he gave a wild cry.

And small wonder. There on the river bank lay the motionless form of his parent, dripping yet with the water of the river. The eyes were closed as if in death. With a moan Dick threw himself forward and caught one of the cold hands within his own. Then he placed his ear to his parent's heart.

"Too late! He is gone!" he wailed. "Poor, poor father, dead after all! Oh, if only I had died with you!" and he sank back utterly overcome.

CHAPTER IX.
MIKE AND THE MULES.

We move in an hour!"

This was the word which was whispered about the boomers' camp shortly after Pawnee Brown's arrival.

The great scout had found it out of the question to attempt to enter the Indian Territory in a direct route from Arkansas City. The government troops were watching the trail, and the soldiers were backed up by the cattle kings' helpers, who would do all in their power to harass the pioneers and make them turn back.

Many a man would have gone ahead with a rush, but Pawnee Brown knew better than to do this. If he was brave, he was also cautious.

"A rush now would mean people killed, horses shot down or poisoned, wagons ditched, harnesses cut up and a thousand and one other disasters," he said. "We must beat the cattle kings at their own game. We will move westward to Honnewell either this afternoon or tonight. Get ready to go on whenever the signal is passed."

"But vot goot vill it do to vait by Honnvell?" questioned Carl Humpendinck, a German boomer.

"We'll not wait very long there," answered Pawnee Brown.

So the word went around that the boomers would move in an hour. This was not actually true, but it was necessary to spread some report of this kind in order to make the slow ones hustle. If left to themselves these few would not have gotten ready in two days.

"It's a move we are afther makin' at last, is it?" burst out Rosy Delaney when Mike brought the news. "Sure, an' Oi'm ready, Moike Delaney, but how are ye to git this wagon out av thet bog hole, Oi dunno."

"Oi'll borry a horse," answered Mike. "It's Jack Rasco will lind me the same."

Mike ran around to where Jack Rasco was in earnest conversation with a stranger who had just come in from town. The stranger had brought a letter from Nellie Winthrop, posted two days before, and saying when she would arrive. The letter caused Rasco not a little worry, as so far the girl had failed to appear.

"I haven't any horse to spare just now, Mike," he said; "but hold on, you can have Billy, the mule, if you wish."

There was a little twinkle in his eyes as he spoke, but Mike didn't see the twinkle and readily accepted the mule and led him over to where his own turn-out stood.

"Moike Delaney, phot kind av a horse do yez call that?" demanded Rosy.

"It's a mule, ye ignoramus," he answered. "An' a good puller, I'll bet me whiskers. Just wait till Oi hitch him beside the tame."

Billy was soon hitched up as Mike desired, and the Irishman proceeded to urge him forward with his short whip.

It was then the fun began. Billy did not appreciate being called upon to do extra work. Instead of pulling, he simply turned around, tangling up and breaking the harness, and began to kick up the black prairie dirt with both hind hoofs.

"Oh, the villain!" spluttered Rosy Delaney, who received the first installment of dirt full in her eyes and mouth. "Moike Delaney, ye made him do that a-purpose!" and she shook her fist at her husband. "Ye bould, bad mon!"

"Oi did not," he ejaculated. "Git back there, ye baste!" he added, and tried to hit Billy with his whip. The knowing mule dodged and, turning swiftly, planted a hoof in Mike's stomach so slickly that the Irishman went heels over head into a nearby puddle.

A shout arose from those standing near.

"Score one round for the mule!"

"Mike, thet summersault war good enough fer a show. Better jine the circus!"

"Oi'll show the mule!" yelled Mike, and rushed in again. But once more Billy turned and got out of the way, and this time he caught the seat of Mike's trousers between his teeth and lifted the frightened man six feet from the ground.

"Don't! Let me down! Somebody save me!" yelled the terrorized son of Erin.

"Rosy! Clemmer! Rasco! Hit him! Shoot him! Make him let go av me! Oi'll be kilt entoirely!"

Outsiders were too much amused to help Mike, but Rosy came to the rescue with a woman's best weapon--a rolling-pin, one she occasionally used in making pies for the family when in camp. Whizz! came the rolling-pin through the air, hitting Billy on the ear. The mule gave a short snort, broke what remained of the harness and scampered off to make a complete circuit of the camp and then fall into his regular place near Jack Rasco's turn-out.

"Want him some more?" asked Jack, who had seen the fun, and was compelled to laugh, in spite of his worry.

"Want him some more, is it?" growled Mike. "Not fer a thousand dollars, Rasco! Yez kin kape the mule, an' be hanged to yez!" and he stalked off to borrow a horse that was warranted to be gentle under the most trying of circumstances.

In the meantime Pawnee Brown was completing his arrangements for moving to Honnewell and then to enter the promised land by way of Bitter Creek and the Secaspie River. Scouts sent out to watch had reported that the cavalry were watching every movement closely, but Pawnee Brown did not dream that Louis Vorlange had overheard what was said at a meeting in the woods, or that this scoundrel had hired Tucker, the cavalryman, to shoot down both himself and Dick Arbuckle.

Presently Jack Rasco found his way to the scout's side.

"Pawnee, if you can spare a little time I would like your advice," he said, and mentioned the letter from Nellie Winthrop. "It's mighty strange the gal don't turn up, ain't it?"

"Perhaps so; but she may have been detained," answered the scout.

At this Rasco shook his head. The bearer of the letter had seen Nellie's name on the hotel register. Something was wrong, he felt sure of it. The letter had contained Nellie's photograph, and he showed it to Pawnee Brown as he asked for permission to leave his work of assisting the boomers to be prepared for a moving in order to pay Arkansas City another visit.

"Go on, Jack. You're my right-hand man, but I'll manage somehow without you," answered the great scout. "A pretty niece for any man to have," and he handed back the photograph, after a somewhat close inspection. Two minutes later found Jack Rasco on his way, to encounter adventures of which he had never imagined.

"A note for you, Pawnee." It was one of the scouts sent out that morning who spoke as he rode up. Pawnee Brown read the communication with interest.

"Come up to the ravine back of Honnewell as soon
as possible," ran the note. "I think the cavalry are
up to some new dodge, or else the cattle men are going
to play us foul. Urgent.
DAN GILBERT."

"I must away, boys!" cried Pawnee Brown, tearing up the note. "Be ready to move, but don't stir until you hear from me," and, giving a few more instructions, he borrowed a fresh horse from Carl Humpendinck and set off on a gallop of twelve miles across the country.

As he covered mile after mile, through woods and over stretches of broad prairie, he could not help but think of his racing mare, Bonnie Bird. How she would have enjoyed this outing, and how she would have covered this ground with her twinkling feet.

"I must find her and find the rascal who stole her!" he muttered. "I wouldn't take twenty thousand dollars for Bonnie," and he meant what he said. The little mare and the great scout were almost inseparable.

The afternoon sun was sinking low when Pawnee Brown struck the outskirts of Honnewell (spelled by some writers, Honeywell). Not caring to be seen in that town by the government agents, who might inform the cavalry that the boomers were moving in that direction, the scout took to a side trail, leading directly for the ravine mentioned in the letter.

Soon he was picking his way down a path covered with brush and loose stones. Upon either side were woods, and so thick no sunlight penetrated, making the spot gloomy and forbidding.

"Now, I suppose I'll have no picnic in finding Dan," he mused. "I'll give the signal."

The shrill cry of a night bird rang out upon the air, and Pawnee Brown listened attentively for a reply. None came, and he repeated the cry, with the same result.

"I'll have to push on a bit further," he thought, and was just about to urge forward his horse when a crashing on the opposite side of the ravine caught his ear. Instinctively he withdrew to the shelter of some brush to learn who the newcomer might be.

He was not kept long in waiting. The sounds came closer and closer, and presently a tall Indian came into view, astride a horse, and carrying an odd-looking burden in his arms.

"Yellow Elk!" almost burst from Pawnee Brown's lips. The Indian he mentioned was a well-known chief, a warrior noted for his many crimes, and a redskin whom the government agent had tried in vain to subdue.

The scout crouched back still further and drew his pistol, for he felt that Yellow Elk was on no lawful errand, and a meeting would most likely mean a fight. Then he made a discovery of still greater importance--to him.

"Bonnie Bird, as sure as shooting! So Yellow Elk is the horse thief. The rascal! I've a good mind to shoot him down where he sits!" He handled his pistol nervously. "What is that he is carrying, wrapped up in his blanket? Ha!"

A murmur of amazement could not now be suppressed. In shifting his burden from one shoulder to the other the Indian had allowed the blanket to fall partly back, and there was now revealed to Pawnee Brown the head and shoulders of a beautiful, but unconscious white girl. Nor was that all. The girl was--Nellie Winthrop!

CHAPTER X.
MR. ARBUCKLE'S STORY.

Father! father! speak to me! Tell me that you are not dead!"

Over and over again did poor Dick repeat these words as he sat by the side of that wet and motionless form on the muddy river bank. The boy's heart seemed to be breaking.

But suddenly there came a change. He saw one of his father's arms quiver. Then came a faint twitching of an eyelid.

"He is alive!" gasped Dick. The joy of the discovery nearly paralyzed him. "Father! father!"

No answer came back, indeed, it was not to be expected. Kneeling over his parent, Dick set to work to resuscitate the almost drowned man.

Fortunately the youth had, during his school days in New York, heard a lecture on what was best to do in just such a case, so he did not labor in ignorance. His treatment was as skillful as memory and his love for his parent could make it, and in less than half an hour he had the satisfaction of seeing his father give a gasp and open his eyes.

"Father, don't you know me?"

"Dick!" came the almost inaudible reply. "Where--where am I?"

"You are safe, father. You fell into the river and came near to drowning."

"Is that so? I did not know there was a river near here."

Mr. Arbuckle was silent for several minutes, during which Dick continued his work and made him as comfortable as possible by wrapping his parent in his own dry coat.

"Where is that rascal?"

"What rascal, father?"

"The man with the red mask--the fellow who struck me down?"

"I do not know. So you were struck down? Where?"

"Just outside of the boomers' camp. Somebody brought me word that Pawnee Brown wanted to see me privately. I went, and a rascal rushed on me and demanded my private papers. I resisted and he struck me down. I know no more than that," and Mr. Arbuckle gave another gasp. His eyes were open, but in them was that uncertain look which Dick had seen before, and which the lad so much dreaded.

"Why, you were struck down last night, father, and several miles from here. You must have come down to the river at a spot above here. Don't you remember that?"

Mortimer Arbuckle tried to think, then shook his head sadly.

"It's all a blur, Dick. You know my head is not as strong as it might be."

"Yes, yes; and you must not try to think too far. So he got your private papers?"

"Yes."

"The ones referring to that silver mine in Colorado?"

"Yes, and all of the others."

At this Dick could not help but groan. The papers were gone--those precious documents by which he and his father had hoped some day to become rich.

The history of the deeds to the silver mine was a curious one. Two years before Mortimer Arbuckle had paid a visit to Creede, Colorado, on business connected with a mining company then forming under the laws of the State of New York.

While in Creede the man had materially assisted an old miner named Burch, who was falling into the hands of a set of swindlers headed by a rascal called Captain Mull.

Mortimer Arbuckle had never met Captain Mull, but he had saved Burch's claim for him, for which the old miner was extremely grateful.

Over a year later Burch had died and left with another old miner the deeds to a new mine of great promise, deeds which had not yet been recorded.

The old miner had forwarded these papers, along with others of importance concerning the exact location of the claim, to Mortimer Arbuckle, and the gentleman had then begun preparations to go to the West and see if the claim was really as valuable as old Burch had imagined.

Dick was just out of school, and would not think of remaining behind, so it was arranged that father and son should go together.

A spell of sickness had detained the father several months. Before this, however, he had hired Jack Rasco to go to Creede with him and assist in locating the new claim.

As Mortimer Arbuckle failed to come West, Jack Rasco returned to the companionship of Pawnee Brown, for, as already stated, he considered himself the great boomer's right-hand man.

At last Mortimer Arbuckle had come on with Dick, to find Rasco had given his word to Pawnee Brown to stick with the boomers until the desired entrance into Oklahoma was effected.

"Yer will hev ter wait, Mr. Arbuckle," Jack had said. "I'm sorry, but I hev given my word ter Pawnee an' I wouldn't break it fer a cool million, thet's me."

"Let us go with the boomers!" Dick had returned enthusiastically. "It will be lots of fun, father, and it will give you a chance to get back your health before you tie yourself down to those silver mine schemes."

And rather against his wishes Mortimer Arbuckle had consented. Dick saw his father was in no mental condition to locate claims, form a new mining company, and do other labor of this sort, and trusted that the days to be spent with the boomers would make him much stronger in both body and mind.

"Do you think the robber thought of the deeds when he robbed you?" went on Dick, after a pause.

"I--I--don't know, Dick. It runs in my mind he spoke of the deeds, but I can't remember for certain."

"He took your money?"

"Every cent." Mortimer Arbuckle gave a groan. "We are now out here penniless, my son."

"No we are not, father. I asked Pawnee Brown for the loan of ten dollars and he gave me twenty, and said I could have more if I needed it."

"A good man--as generous as he is brave," murmured Mortimer Arbuckle. "Would the world had more of such fellows."

"Pawnee Brown and Jack Rasco are the best fellows in the world!" answered the youth. "But, come, let me carry you to yonder house, where you can get dry and also get something to eat."

He assisted his parent to his feet, then lifted the man to his back and started off. A backwoodsman saw him coming, and ran to meet him. Soon Mortimer Arbuckle was in the house and lying tucked in on a warm couch.

A relapse followed, coming almost immediately after father and son had exchanged stories and detail. In alarm Dick sent off the backwoodsman for a doctor. The medical man was half an hour in coming. After a thorough examination he looked grave.

"The man must be kept absolutely quiet," he said. "If you have been talking to him it has done him more harm than good. You had better go away and leave him among strangers."

In a further conversation Dick learned that the backwoodsman, Peter Day, and his wife were ready to take charge of the invalid for fair pay, and could be trusted to do their best, and it was arranged to leave Mr. Arbuckle at the house, while Dick returned to camp, hunted up Pawnee Brown and Jack Rasco and tried to get on the track of the man of the red mask.

"And if I ever get hold of him I'll--I'll--mash him," said Dick, and the look on his youthful but stern face told that he meant just what he said. The western idea of shooting had not yet entered his mind, but woe to Louis Vorlange if his villainy was once unmasked.

"Do not worry about me, father," said Dick taking his departure. "I will take care of myself, and I am sure that either Pawnee Brown, Jack Rasco or myself can get on the track of the rascal who robbed and struck you down."

"Be cautious, Dick," murmured the sick man. "Be cautious--for you are all the world to me!" and he kissed his son affectionately.

"Who could have attacked father?" he murmured, half aloud. "It was a dastardly thing to do. I must find out, even if I have to remain in the city. But who knows but what it was one of the boomers? Perhaps the man saw father had money and only asked about his papers to put him off the track. As a rule, the boomers are as honest as men can be, but there are several hang-dog faces among them."

Dick had covered a distance of half a mile and was within sight of the spot where he had been rescued by Pawnee Brown from a watery grave, when a murmur of voices broke upon his ear, coming from a thicket down by the river bank.

The murmur grew louder and he paused to listen.

Suddenly two pistol shots rang out, followed by a cry of pain and rage. There was a brief silence, then came the words which made Dick's heart almost stop beating:

"Now I'll fix you for helping to run me out of town, Jack Rasco! I never forget my enemies!"

CHAPTER XI.
A STRANGE LETTER.

To return to Pawnee Brown at the time when he made the double discovery that Yellow Elk, the rascally Indian, was riding his stolen mare, Bonnie Bird, and had as his fair captive Nellie Winthrop, Jack Rasco's niece.

For the moment the great scout was nearly dum founded by the revelation. He had not met Yellow Elk for several months, and had imagined that the Indian chief was safe within the territorial reservation allotted to him and his tribe.

As Yellow Elk shifted his fair burden, Nellie Winthrop's eyes opened and she started up in alarm.

"Oh, you beast! Let me go!" she screamed faintly. She was about to say more, but Yellow Elk clapped a dirty hand over her mouth and silenced her.

"No speak more," he muttered in his broken English. "White girl speak too much."

"But--but where are you taking me? This is not the boomers' camp."

"We come to camp soon--girl in too much hurry," rejoined the wily redskin.

"I was told the camp was but a short distance out of town."

"Camp he move. Pawnee Brown not safe near big town," went on Yellow Elk.

"You're a good one for fairy tales," was the boomer's silent comment. He had withdrawn to the shelter of the thick brush and sat his steed like a statue, while his pistol was ready for use, with his forefinger upon the trigger.

"But--but--what happened to me?" went on Nellie, struggling to sit up, while Yellow Elk held her back.

"White girl lose breath and shut eyes," was the answer, meaning that Nellie had fainted. "No more fight--Yellow Elk no hurt her."

"I will go no further with you--I do not believe your story!" cried Nellie. "Let me down."

At these words the face of the Indian chief grew dark, and he muttered several words in his own language which Nellie did not understand, but which Pawnee Brown made out to be that the White Bird was too sweet to be lost so easily, he must take her to his cave in the mountains.

"Will you?" murmured Pawnee Brown. "Well, maybe, but not if I know it."

The mentioning of a cave in the mountains made Pawnee Brown curious. Did Yellow Elk have such a hiding place? Where was it located, and was the Indian chief its only user?

"Perhaps some more of these reds have broken loose," he thought. "I would like to investigate. Who knows but what the cavalrymen are after them and not the boomers, as Dan Gilbert imagined."

A brief consideration of the subject and his mind was made up. So long as the Indian did not offer positive harm to Nellie Winthrop he would not expose himself, but follow on behind, in hope of locating the cave and learning more of Yellow Elk's intended movements.

"Let me go, I say!" cried Nellie, but the Indian chief merely shook his head.

"White girl be no fool. Indian friend; no hurt one hair of her head. Soon we be in camp and she will see what a friend Yellow Elk has been."

At this Nellie shook her head. That painted and dirty face was far too repulsive to be trusted. But there was no help for it; the Indian held her as in a vise, and she was forced to submit.

Moving along the trail, Indian and horse passed within a dozen feet of where Pawnee Brown sat, still as silent as a block of marble. It was a trying moment. What if the horse he rode should make a noise, or if his own Bonnie Bird should instinctively discover him and give the alarm?

"Poor Bonnie Bird, to have to carry a dirty redskin," thought the boomer. The ears of the beautiful mare went up as she drew close, and she appeared to hesitate. But Yellow Elk urged her along by several punches in the ribs, and in a moment more the danger of discovery just then was past.

On went the tall Indian along the ravine, peering cautiously ahead, with one hand around Nellie's waist and the other holding the reins and his pistol. He knew he was on a dangerous mission, and he stood ready, if unmasked, to sell his worthless life dearly.

Pawnee Brown followed at a distance of a hundred feet, taking care to pick his way so that his horse's hoofs should strike only the dirt and soft moss, and that the brush growing among the tall trees should screen him as much as possible.

Presently he saw the Indian halt and stare long and hard at a tall pine growing in front of a large flat rock.

"Wonder if he has missed his way?" mused the scout, but a moment later Yellow Elk proceeded onward, faster than ever.

Coming up to the pine, Pawnee Brown saw instantly what had attracted the redskin's attention. There was a blaze on the tree six inches square, and on the blaze was written in charcoal:

10 f. E. D. G.

"Hullo, a message from Dan," he cried, half aloud. He had read the strange marking without difficulty. It ran as follows:

"Ten feet east.

DAN GILBERT."

Pacing off the ten feet in the direction indicated, Pawnee Brown located a flat rock. Raising this, he uncovered a small, circular hole, in the centre of which lay a leaf torn from a note book, on which was written:

"I write this to notify Pawnee Brown or any of my other friends that I have gone up the ravine on the trail of half a dozen cavalry scouts who are up here, not only to watch for boomers, but also to try and locate several Indians who have left the reservation without permission. I will be back soon.   DAN GILBERT."

The boomer read the note with interest. Then he hastily scribbled off the answer:

"Have read the note that was left. Am following Yellow Elk, who stole my mare and has Jack Rasco's niece a captive. Yellow Elk is bound for some cave in the mountains.   PAWNEE BROWN."

The answer finished, the boomer placed it in the hole, let back the flat rock and wrote on the blaze of the tree, under Dan Gilbert's initials:

P. B.

CHAPTER XII.
YELLOW ELK.

The writing of the answer to Gilbert's communication had taken several minutes, and now Yellow Elk was entirely out of sight. But Pawnee Brown was certain of the trail the Indian had taken, and by a little faster riding soon brought the rascal again into view.

Yellow Elk was now descending into a valley bound on the north by a rolling hill and on the south by a cliff varying from twenty to forty feet in height. Even at a distance Pawnee Brown could see that the Indian was having considerable trouble with Nellie Winthrop, who felt now assured that her first suspicions were correct and that Yellow Elk had taken her far from the boomers' camp.

"I will not go with you!" cried the girl, and did her best to break from the warrior's grasp. But Yellow Elk's hold was a good one, and she only succeeded in tearing her dress.

"We be dare in few minutes now," replied the redskin. "Den all be right--you wait and see."

"I won't go with you--let me down!" screamed Nellie, but he silenced her by a fierce gesture which made the boomer's blood boil. It was only by the exercise of all his will power that the great scout kept himself from shooting down Yellow Elk on the spot.

The end of the long cliff was almost reached when the Indian chief reined up the mare and sprang to the ground, still holding Nellie tight. As he held the girl by the wrist with one hand he led Bonnie Bird forward with the other. In a few seconds, girl, mare and Indian had disappeared from view in the midst of a thick fringe of bushes.

They had scarcely vanished when Pawnee Brown was on the ground and had tethered his horse in a little grove of pines a hundred feet away. This done, he stole forward to what he felt must be the mouth of the cave Yellow Elk had mentioned.

The great scout knew he was on delicate and dangerous ground. There was no telling how many Indians beside Yellow Elk there might be in the vicinity, who had left the reservation without permission; it was likely all who were there would be in war paint ready to kill him on sight.

"The reds who train with Yellow Elk are not to be trusted," he muttered. "Yellow Elk wouldn't like anything better than to scalp me just for a taste of his old blood-thirsty days. Making a 'good Indian' out of such a fellow is all nonsense--it simply can't be done."

Pawnee Brown had dropped down in the long grass and was now wiggling along like a snake through the bushes and between the rocks. Soon the entrance to the cave was gained, hidden by more bushes. He hesitated, looked to see that his pistol was all right, shoved the bushes aside and slipped within.

It was so dark inside that for a moment he could distinguish nothing. But his ears were on the alert and he heard the footsteps of Yellow Elk resounding at a distance of fully fifty yards. He could hear nothing of Nellie, and rightfully concluded that the Indian had been compelled to pick her up and carry her.

An instant later he stumbled close to his mare. Bonnie Bird recognized him with a snort of joy.

"Sh-sh!" he said softly, and the gentle animal understood and made no further sound. But she gladly rubbed her soft nose up and down his neck to signify her pleasure.

"Good Bonnie Bird," he whispered. "I'll be with you soon again," and went on after Yellow Elk.

The Indian had now come to a halt and was striking a match. Soon some dry brush was set on fire and the redskin heaped upon it some stout tree branches, for the air in the cave was chilly.

"Now me and white girl have long talk," said Yellow Elk, as he motioned Nellie to a seat.

"Where is the boomers' camp?" she faltered, hardly knowing how to answer him.

"Camp ten miles from here," came the short reply. "You here all alone with

Yellow Elk."

At this the frightened girl gave a scream of terror.

"You base wretch!" she sobbed. "Take me back at once."

"No take back--Yellow Elk no fool. White girl stay here--make Yellow Elk good squaw, maybe," and he grinned into her pretty face.

But now an interruption came which all but stunned Yellow Elk. Leaping from his hiding place, Pawnee Brown pounced upon the redskin, caught him by the throat and hurled him backward and almost into the midst of the fire!

"You miserable dog!" came from the scout's lips.

"Oh, sir, save me from that Indian!" came from Nellie, as she quickly turned to the man she felt sure would assist her.

"I will, Miss Winthrop, don't fear," answered Pawnee Brown. "So, Yellow Elk, we meet again. I reckon you remember the man who kicked you all around the agency two years ago because you tried to steal his new pair of boots?"

"Ugh!" grunted Yellow Elk. He had just managed to scramble out of the fire, and was beating out the flames which had caught on a fringe of his garments. "Pawnee Brown."

He muttered a fierce imprecation in his native tongue. Then, before Pawnee Brown could stop him his pistol flashed in the fire-light. He took aim at the scout's head and fired.

But though the action of the Indian chief was quick, the movement of the boomer was quicker. Many times had he been under fire, and he had learned to drop when occasion required as rapidly as it could be done.

With the pressure upon the pistol trigger he went down like a flash and the bullet intended for his head merely grazed the top of his hat and flattened itself upon the cave wall opposite.

"Bah!" hissed Yellow Elk, when he saw how he had missed. He attempted to take him once more, but now Pawnee Brown hurled himself on the redskin, turning the barrel of the weapon aside, and both went to the stone flooring with a crash. Nellie Winthrop let out a shriek of terror.

"Do not let him shoot you! Make him throw the pistol away!" she cried, as she wrung her hands. She would have liked to assist Pawnee Brown, but could not see how it could just then be done.

CHAPTER XIII.
NELLIE'S FLIGHT.

Over and over on the stone flooring rolled the boomer and his red enemy, now close to the fire and again off to one side, where there was a slight hollow still wet from the recent storm.

Pawnee Brown had Yellow Elk by the throat and across the back, while the Indian held his antagonist by the shoulder with one hand, while trying to beat his brains out with the pistol that was in the other.

Once Yellow Elk succeeded in getting in a glancing blow, which drew blood, but did no great harm. But now Pawnee Brown's grip was tightening. The redskin was choking. His eyes bulged from their sockets and his tongue hung out several inches.

"Ugh!" gasped the Indian chief. In vain he tried to shake off that grip. It was like that of a bulldog and could not be loosened. He struck out wildly, but the pistol butt only landed upon Pawnee Brown's shoulder, a shoulder that was as tough as iron and could stand any amount of pounding.

Suddenly the tactics of the Indian changed. Knowing that he was in immediate danger of death by choking, and feeling how unlikely it was that he could throw off his assailant, he let fall his pistol and caught the boomer around the body. Then he began to roll toward the fire, which was now blazing up more brightly than ever.

The scout saw the redskin's intention instantly, but before he could stop it both he and his enemy were close to the flames.

"Me die you die too!" hissed Yellow Elk, and gave another roll, which took both himself and Pawnee Brown into the very edge of the blaze.

"Take care! You will be burnt up!" cried Nellie Winthrop, and gave a scream. Rushing forward, she caught Pawnee Brown by the arm and attempted to draw him back.

But of this there was no need, for the great scout had already changed his tactics, feeling convinced that to choke Yellow Elk was now impossible. His hand left the redskin's throat, to double up and sail forth into a crushing blow, which took the Indian chief beneath the eyes and made him see more stars than were ever beheld in the blue canopy of heaven. As Yellow Elk fell back Pawnee Brown did likewise, but in a different direction.

The Indian was now in the midst of the flames and the cry he let out was truly blood-curdling. Excited as he was, Pawnee Brown did not let the intonation of that cry escape him. Understanding the Indian language well, he knew it was more than a cry of terror or pain, it was a call for help! Other Indians must be somewhere in the vicinity.

"You had better run for it!" he said, turning to Nellie. "Mount my horse--the mare the Indian had--and ride down the ravine."

"Run?" she faltered.

"Yes, and hurry. Hark! As I thought! Other Indians are coming!"

The boomer was right. The footsteps sounded from the opposite end of the cave, which had two entrances, similar to each other.

By this time Yellow Elk had rolled out of the fire and was dancing around like a madman, trying to beat out the flames which had communicated to his clothing.

As Nellie ran off, Pawnee Brown drew his pistol, resolved to not only defend himself but cover the girl's retreat as well.

Little did he dream of the fresh perils which awaited Nellie. What those perils were the immediate chapters which follow will relate.

As Yellow Elk danced around, Pawnee Brown leveled his revolver at him.

Crack! went the weapon and the Indian chief fell back with a wound through his shoulder. The flickering of the fire-light had saved him from death.

A cry that was little less than a war whoop now sounded out, and with this four other Indians appeared, two whom Pawnee Brown had before seen in Yellow Elk's company and two who were utter strangers to him.

"Capture the white dog!" howled Yellow Elk, in his native tongue. "Shoot the dog down!"

"Pawnee Brown!" grunted one of the newcomers, and up went several pistols.

The scout fired at the same time, and one of the strange Indians threw up his hands and fell lifeless. But the bullet this Indian had sent on its mission struck the boomer across the forehead and sent the scout to the flooring of the cave senseless.

When Pawnee Brown came to a clear mind again he found himself aching in every portion of his body, for in their usual custom the Indians on finding him helpless had each taken their turn at kicking him to suit their pleasure, Yellow Elk especially delighting in this cruel performance.

The scout was bound tightly with a lariat which started from his feet and was wound and crossed up to his very neck, making body, legs and arms as stiff as those of an Egyptian mummy. He lay on the cave flooring not a dozen feet from the fire, which Yellow Elk was in the act of replenishing.

As he opened his eyes one of the other Indians, Spotted Nose by name, stopped in front of him. The scout instantly closed his eyes again, but it was too late.

"You all right," cried Spotted Nose, and gave him a sharp kick in the side.

"Well I won't be if you keep on kicking me," replied the boomer, as cheerfully as he could, although it must be admitted he was much disturbed. He glanced around and was relieved to see that Nellie was nowhere in sight.

Yellow Elk now came up and also kicked the prostrate scout.

"You heap dirty dog!" he exclaimed, his face full of bitter hatred. "You shoot me--you die for dat."

"I suppose I will--if you have the saying of that, Yellow Elk. But perhaps you won't dare to kill me."

"Why not Indian dare? Indian dare anything," growled Yellow Elk.

"My friends are not far off--they will soon come here, and if you harm me it will go hard with you."

At this all of the Indians laughed.

"No white man around here--we on guard all time," said Spotted Nose.

"On guard, eh? And yet you didn't see me come in, Dirty Nose?"

"Spotted Nose did see Pawnee Brown," was the answer; but this was a falsehood. An Indian hates to admit that he has been in any manner outwitted by a white man.

"You tell a good story, Dirty Nose." Pawnee Brown turned to Yellow Elk. "Yellow, how did you run across that girl?"

"Yellow Elk no tell his secrets," came the answer. "Pawnee Brown fool to ask. Pawnee Brown think him heap sly, like fox, but him sly only like cow!" This produced another laugh, for the Indians from the Indian Territory are not as stolid as were their forefathers, and thoroughly enjoy their own rude manner of joking.

Presently Yellow Elk turned to his companions and spoke to them in an undertone. A moment later he sped away, but whether in pursuit of Nellie Winthrop or not, Pawnee Brown could not tell.

The Indian chief was gone fully an hour, and came back looking unusually grave.

Pawnee Brown had tried in vain to get Spotted Nose and the other Indian to talk--to tell him why they had left the reservation. Not one would speak further than to tell him to keep quiet.

On returning, Yellow Elk at once set to work to rig up an upright pole from the floor to the ceiling of the cave, using a heavy tree branch for the purpose. The upright was placed close to where the smoke from the fire found a vent through several large cracks in the ceiling, and the boomer watched these proceedings with much alarm.

The Indians were erecting a fire-stake, such as they had used in the wild west when some victim was to be roasted alive!

"Heavens! can that be meant for me?" was the question he asked himself.

The stake planted and fastened firmly, Yellow Elk heaped some fresh, dry brush around its bottom and then came up to Pawnee Brown.

"Pawnee Brown see the fire-stake?" he asked, his savage eyes gleaming like two stars.

"I do, Yellow. Who is it for?"

"Why does Pawnee Brown ask? Does he not deserve death?"

"I suppose I do--according to your notion."

"Pawnee Brown shall burn--he shall burn slowly," went on Yellow Elk, meaning that he would make the great scout's torture last as long as possible.

"Your training on the reservation hasn't civilized you much, Yellow, if that's the way you feel about it."

"I hate white man--all of them," grumbled the Indian chief. "They take all my land away and put me in a little yard to live. I would kill all white man if could," and he grated his teeth.

A moment later Yellow Elk nodded to the other Indians and all leaped forward and bound Pawnee Brown fast to the fire-stake. This done the redskins heaped the brush around the scout's feet.

"Now the dirty white dog can die!" hissed Yellow Elk, as he advanced with a torch. "He can pray, but the white man's Great Father cannot save him! He must burn until his bones are as charcoal!"

And so speaking Yellow Elk thrust the torch into the dry brush and set it on fire!

CHAPTER XIV.
DICK TO THE RESCUE.

That man is going to shoot Jack Rasco!"

Such was the thought which rushed into Dick Arbuckle's mind as he heard the fatal words spoken in the woods near the river bank.

He could not see either of the men, but he felt tolerably certain in his mind that Rasco's assailant was Stillwater, the gambler, who had been run out of Arkansas City by Pawnee Brown, Rasco, Clemmer and a dozen others.

"Would you kill me?" came in Rasco's voice. The boomer was concerned and was doing his best to gain time, in the hope that something would turn up to his advantage.

"Kill you?" sneered Stillwater. "Do you think I'm going to put up with the way I've been treated? Not much! I had a fine thing in Arkansas City--something worth a thousand a week to me, and you and your friends spoiled it all. I'm going to settle with you, and after that I shall hunt up Pawnee Brown and the rest and settle with them, also."

"You'll have your hands full a-settlin' with Pawnee."

"Bah! I am not afraid of him. He had me foul over to the Golden Pick, but I'll be careful when next we meet. But I'll not waste time with you here, Rasco. I've got you alone and 'dead men tell no tales.'"

"Alone?" Jack Rasco began to smile. "You're mistaken. Look behind you."

Stillwater started, but did not look back.

"That's an old dodge, Rasco, but you can't work it off on me. I have you alone and I'm going to end the business right here."

"Not yet!" cried a youthful voice behind Stillwater, and crash! down came a heavy stick, hitting the gambler squarely upon the head and sending him with a thud to the earth.

As Stillwater went down, Rasco leaped forward and came down upon him. But this movement was useless. The rascal was more than three-quarters knocked out and lay for several minutes helpless.

"I owe you one fer that, Dick Arbuckle!" cried Rasco, gratefully. "Yer came in the nick o' time!" Now the peril was over the boomer dropped back into his own peculiar manner of speech.

"I am glad I happened this way," returned Dick, as he drew a long breath. "Gosh! what a lot of excitement we are passing through out here! More than I experienced in all my life in New York."

"The West is the place fer stirrin' times, lad." Jack Rasco turned to his prostrate foe. "Wall, Stillwater, do yer think it war a trick now, tellin' yer ter look behind yer?"

The rascal answered with a groan.

"My head is split in two!" he cried. "Who struck me? What, that boy? I'll remember you, youngster, and some day----" He did not finish.

"I ain't done with yer yet, Stillwater," said Rasco. "You war goin' ter shoot me. I reckon turn about is fair play, ain't it?"

"Would you--you shoot me--now?" faltered the card sharp. At the bottom of his heart he was a coward.

"Why not?"

"I wasn't going to do it, Rasco--I was only--only scaring you."

"Thet's a whopper--made outer the hull cloth, Stillwater. Yer war going ter shoot me--an' I'm a-goin' ter be jess as accommodatin'," and on the sly Rasco winked at Dick who was much relieved to think the boomer did not really intend to carry out his blood-thirsty design.

The face of Stillwater grew as white as a sheet and he trembled from head to foot.

"Don't! don't you do it! Let me off, and I'll give you all the money I have with me."

"It won't do, Stillwater."

"It's nearly a thousand dollars. Take every cent of it and let me go!"

The gambler fairly grovelled at Jack Rasco's feet. His horror of dying was something fearful to contemplate.

"I'll give yer one chance, Stillwater," said Rasco, in deep disgust, and at once the rascal's face took on a look of hope. "Yer ain't fit ter die, an' thet's why I say it. Promise ter let me an' my friends alone in the future."

"I promise."

"Promise ter give up cheatin' at cards. If yer don't, some day it will be the death of yer."

"I'll never cheat again."

"All right, I'll take yer at yer word. Now come on down to the river."

"What for?"

"You hev got ter swim across to the other side whar yer belong. Decent folks ain't a-goin' ter have yer over here."

Again Stillwater was much disturbed. But Jack Rasco was firm, and soon the trio were down by the water's edge. Still pale, the gambler plunged into the river and struck out for the opposite shore. It was a hard battle against that current, but presently Rasco and Dick saw him wade out at the other side. He shook his fist at them savagely, then disappeared like a flash into the woods.

"He'll not keep any of his promises," said Dick.

"Keep 'em? Yer didn't expect it o' thet viper, lad? No, he's an enemy to the death. But whar did yer come from, and have yer found out anything about yer poor father?"

Dick's story was soon told, to which Rasco listened with much interest.

"I don't believe a boomer would rob yer father," said he, reflectively. "Like as not it war somebody who followed yer from New York--some man as knew the value of them air minin' deeds."

"Well, I'll go back to camp and make a search, anyway, Rasco. But what brought you here?"

"I'm lookin' fer my niece, Nellie Winthrop."

And Rasco told of the letter received and of how Nellie was missing and no trace of her could be found anywhere. Dick was almost as much disturbed as Rasco, for he still carried in his mind a picture of the beautiful girl he had saved from Juan Donomez's insults.

"Can the Mexican have waylaid her?" he asked.

"Perhaps," said the man of the plains. "But I've hunted the city high and low."

A short while after the two found themselves in the town once more. Nellie had put up at the Commercial Hotel, and to this hostelry they made their way and entered the office.

"No news of the young lady," said the clerk in charge, who had been interviewed before. "I am quite certain she started for the boomers' camp on horseback."

Rasco heaved a sigh.

"Might as well go back," he said to Dick, then as he saw the boy start he continued: "What's up? Do yer see anything of her?"

"No, Rasco. But look at that man, the fellow sitting down by the corner table in the reading room, he with the brown hat."

"I see him. What of him?"

"He's from New York--a fellow who used to come sneaking around father's office, trying to gather information about mining shares."

"Gee shoo, Dick! Yer don't mean it!" Jack Rasco was all attention instantly. "Maybe he's the rascal as knocked yer dad over?"

"Perhaps. If I--There is a man joining him."

"I've seen thet chap afore. 'Pears ter me he works fer the government."

"Do you know his name?"

"No. Wot's the other fellow's handle?"

"Dike Powell. He is known as a Wall street sharper. I wish I could hear what the two have to say to each other. Yet I don't want Dike Powell to see me."

"It's easy enough, lad. Thar's a window close to the table, an' it's open. We'll walk out on the veranda, and get under the opening. Come."

In a second more they were outside. Tiptoeing their way across the veranda, which was deserted, they soon found themselves close to the open window mentioned.

"And so that is settled," they heard the man from New York remark. "I am glad to hear it, Vorlange."

Vorlange! Dick started and so did Jack Rasco. The boy was trying to think where he had heard it before. Ah, he had it now. Many and many a time had he heard his parent murmur that name in his sleep, and the name was coupled with many other things, dreadful to remember. Surely there was some awful mystery here. What made his father mutter that name in his dreams, and why at such time was he talking of murder and hanging, and sobbing that he was innocent? A cold chill crept down the boy's backbone. Was the heart of that secret to be laid bare at last?

CHAPTER XV.
AN IMPORTANT CONVERSATION.

Yes, it's settled, Powell; and as soon as we are done here with the boomers, I'll get to work and find out what the claim is worth."

"How about being shadowed in the affair?"

"I'm not afraid--I'm laying my plans too well," answered Louis Vorlange. "I would go ahead at once, but to throw up my position under the government just now might excite suspicions."

"Have you the papers with you?"

"No; I left them at the cavalry camp. They are too valuable to carry in one's coat pocket."

"Supposing the camp moves?"

"I have my belongings secreted in a nearby cave where they are as safe as in a deposit vault of a bank."

"Well, Vorlange, what am I to do now I am out here?"

"Remain in Arkansas City for the present and take it easy."

"You promised me a hundred dollars on my arrival."

"And there it is."

There was the rustle of bank notes.

"New money, eh?" was Dike Powell's comment. "Been printing some out here?"

"Not much. I know better than to go into the counterfeiting business."

Dick clutched Rasco's arm. The youth's face was full of concern.

"My father's money was in new bills," he whispered into his companion's ear. Rasco nodded, but quickly motioned for silence.

"I reckon this is drinks on me," said Powell, arising. "Come down to the bar before you go back to the cavalry camp."

"I'm in a hurry, Powell, but I'll take one glass," concluded Louis Vorlange, and the two men hurried from the reading-room.

"He is the man--I feel certain of it!" burst from Dick's lips, when he felt safe to speak. "Rasco, there is some mystery here. My father----" He stopped short and bit his lip.

"I know wot's in yer mind, Dick. I've heard yer father go on in his sleep, and war talkin' ter Pawnee Brown about it. An' Pawnee knows this air Vorlange. The two air enemies from school days. Pawnee said Vorlange wasn't squar nohow!"

"He is evidently in the employ of the government."

"Yes; a land-office spy, now workin' ag'in the boomers fer the cavalry as intends ter keep us out of Oklahoma."

"It will be hard to bring such a man to justice, without some direct evidence against him, Rasco."

"Don't yer try ter do it--yet, lad. Take my advice an' watch him. An' afore yer come down on him yer hed better question yer father about Vorlange."

At this Dick winced.

"Rasco, my father's manner is against him--I know that. But I'm certain he never committed a crime in his life."

"I believes yer, Dick. Yer father's a gentleman, every inch o' him; I seed thet the fust I clapped eyes on him. But knowin' the truth is one thing an' provin' it is another, especially in the wild west. This air Vorlange may hev yer father in a mighty tight hole, and if you show him up as the thief who stole the deeds an' the money, he may turn on yer dad and squeeze him mightily, see?"

"I see. But what shall I do just now?"

"Follow Vorlange and spy on to him all yer can. It ain't no ust ter hurry matters, with your father flat on his back. Powell will remain here and Vorlange will be with the cavalry, so yer will know whar ter clap eyes on ter both of 'em if it's necessary."

A moment's reflection convinced Dick that this was sound advice, and he said he would follow it, mentally resolved not to accuse Vorlange of anything until he had gotten his parent to confess to the true state of affairs.

By this time the boy and the man of the plains had left the veranda and walked around to where Rasco had left his horse. A moment later they saw Louis Vorlange hurry from the barroom of the hotel, leap upon his own animal, and strike out of town in a westerly direction.

"If I had a horse I'd follow him," began Dick, when Rasco motioned the youth to hop up behind. Soon they were riding after Vorlange, but not close enough to allow the spy to imagine that he was being followed.

"If you go after him you'll get no chance to hunt up your niece," began Dick, when the city was left behind.

"That's true, lad." Jack Rasco's face grew troubled. "I don't know wot's best ter do. It ain't fair ter let yer follow Vorlange alone; an' with only one hoss----hullo, wot does this mean? Carl Humpendinck, an' wavin' his hand to us like he war crazy."

Rasco had discovered the German boomer sweeping up a side trail. Humpendinck had made out Rasco but a second before and now shouted for the man of the plains to halt.

"What is it, Dutchy?" called out Rasco, when they were within speaking distance.

"Vot ist it? Donner und blitzen, Rasco, it vos der vorst news vot efer you heard!" burst from Carl Humpendinck's lips. "I chust here him apout quarter of an hour ago, und I ride der horse's legs off ter told yer."

"But what is it--out with it?"

"It's apout dot girl you vos lookin' for. Rosy Delaney, dot Irish vomans vot haf such a long tongue got, she tole me der sthory. Gott im himmel! it vos dreadful!"

"But tell me what it is, Dutchy!" exploded Rasco. "Wot is dreadful?"

"Der sthory she tole--I can's most believe him."

"See here, out with the whole thing, or I'll swat yer one on the cocoanut, Humpendinck!" roared Rasco. "Yer as long-winded ez a mule thet's gone blind."

"Gracious, Rasco, you vouldn't hit me, afther I ride me dree miles und more ter tole you?" wailed the German, reproachfully. "I dink me you vos mine pest friend, next to Pawnee Prown, ain't it?"

"There'll be a dead Dutchman here in another minute if yer don't open up clear down ter the bottom!" howled Rasco, who had never before suffered such exasperation.

"Tell us the exact trouble," put in Dick, calmly. He saw that exciting Humpendinck still more would do no good.

"Der Indian haf carried dot girl avay!" exploded Humpendinck.

"Carried the girl away!" ejaculated Dick.

"My Nellie?" yelled Rasco.

"Dot's it, Rasco. Ain't it awful! Dot Irish vomans seen dot Indian mit dot girl in his arms, flying der trail ofer like a biece of baber pefore a cyclone alretty!"

"Humpendinck, are you telling the truth?"

"I vos tole you vot dot Irish vomans tole me. Mike Delaney und dree udder mans vos lookin' for you."

On the instant Louis Vorlange was forgotten, not only by Rasco, ut also by Dick. It made both shudder to think that Nellie had been carried off by a redskin. They turned into the trail from which Humpendinck had emerged, and were soon on their way to the camp.

Here Rosy Delaney was found very much disturbed. She came up to Rasco wringing her hands.

"To think o' the red rascal a-takin' thet young leddy off!" she cried. "I know her by thet photygraph! Och, the villain! An' it moight have been Rosy Delaney, bad cess to him!"

"Show me the exact trail he followed," said Rasco, and this the Irish woman did willingly. Soon Rasco was tearing over the prairie, followed by Humpendinck, Delaney, Clemmer and by Dick, who borrowed a horse from another boomer.

The trail left by Yellow Elk was easily followed to the vicinity of Honnewell, but here it led away to the southwest and was swallowed up among the bushes and rocks leading down into the ravine previously mentioned.

"Oi reckon thot's the trail," said Delaney, after an examination.

"And I vos dink dot ist der trail," put in Humpendinck.

"An' I calkerlate this is the trail," added Cal Clemmer.

Each pointed in a different direction, while Rasco and Dick were of the opinion that none of them were right and that the trail led up the ravine, just as it really did.

An interruption now occurred. There was a stir in the bushes above their heads, and an elderly scout peered down upon them, rifle in hand.

"Hullo, Jack Rasco, wot's the best word? Whar is Pawnee Brown?"

"Dan Gilbert!" cried Rasco. "Come down, Pawnee ought to be somewhere about here."

In a moment more Dan Gilbert, a heavy-set, pleasant-looking frontiersman, stood among them. A hasty consultation immediately followed. Dan Gilbert was on his way back to where he had left the blaze on the tree, and it was decided that Rasco and Dick should accompany him, while Clemmer, Delaney and Humpendinck went to reconnoitre in the opposite direction. A double pistol shot from either party was to bring the other to its aid.

In less than five minutes the first party was on its way to the blazed tree. Dan Gilbert feeling certain that if Pawnee Brown had passed that way he must have seen the sign and left word of his own.

"If Pawnee was down here you can bet he spotted that Injun if he came within a hundred yards of him," said Gilbert. "He can smell a red like a cat can smell a rat."

The tree reached, the frontiersman threw back the flat rock and brought forth the message left by the great scout. He read it aloud.

"Following Yellow Elk!" cried Jack Rasco. "I know the rascal! And it was he as stole my gal! Jess wait till I git my hand on his windpipe, thet's all! Whar's thet cave, Gilbert?"

"I don't know, but it must be somewhere up the ravine. Come on."

And away went the trio, on the hunt for Yellow Elk, Pawnee Brown and poor Nellie Winthrop.

CHAPTER XVI.
ATTACKED BY A WILDCAT.

Y ou fiend!"

This was all Pawnee Brown could say, as with a face full of bitter hatred Yellow Elk advanced and applied the torch to the dry brush which encircled his feet.

In vain the great scout endeavored to wrench himself free from the fire-stake. Yellow Elk and his followers had done their work well and he was held as in a vise.

"Pawnee Brown shall burn slowly," said the Indian chief, hoping to make the scout show the white feather. "Yellow Elk will watch that the fire does not mount to his body too quickly."

"If you want to kill me why don't you put a bullet through my heart and have done with it," said the boomer as coolly as he could. The fire was now burning around his feet and ankles and the pain was increasing with every second of time.

"White man shall learn what it is to suffer," said Spotted Nose. "He killed my friend, the Little Mule."

"Your friend tried to take my life."

"Bah! say no more but burn! burn!" hissed Yellow Elk.

And with a stick he shoved the flaming brush closer in around the scout's legs.

It was a fearful moment--a moment in which Pawnee Brown's life hung by a single thread. The flames were leaping up all around him. He closed his eyes and half murmured a prayer for divine aid.

Crack! bang! crack! Two pistol shots and the report of a rifle echoed throughout the cave, and as Pawnee Brown opened his eyes in astonishment Spotted Nose threw up his arms and fell forward in the flames at his feet, dead! The Indian who had been with Spotted Nose also went down, mortally wounded, while Yellow Elk was hit in the left arm.

"Down with the reds!" came in the ringing voice of Jack Rasco, and he appeared from out of a cloud of smoke, closely followed by Dan Gilbert and Dick. "Pawnee! Am I in time? I hope ter Heaven I am!"

"Jack!" cried the great scout. A slash of Rasco's hunting knife and he was free. "Good for you!" and then Pawnee Brown had his hands full for several minutes beating out the flames which had ignited his boot soles and the bottoms of his trousers.

"We plugged the three of 'em," said Gilbert. "I knocked thet one," and he pointed to the Indian who was breathing his last.

"I hit the Indian with the yellow plume," put in Dick, and he could not help but shudder.

"That was Yellow Elk," said Rasco. "But whar is he now?"

All the white men turned quickly, looking up and down the cave. It was useless. Yellow Elk had disappeared.

"He must not escape!" cried Pawnee Brown. "I have an account to settle with him for starting that fire."

"But whar is Nellie?" asked Rasco, impatiently, looking around with a falling face.

"She ran away when the other Indians came to Yellow Elk's assistance," answered Pawnee Brown, and in a few hurried words he told his story.

"Then she can't be far off."

"Let us hunt for her at once," cried Dick, and his enthusiasm made the men laugh, at which the boy blushed furiously.

"Never mind, Dick, yer don't think no more of her nor I do," said Rasco. "Which way, Pawnee?"

"This way, boys." The scout turned to the Indian who had been wounded. "Dead as a door nail. Pity it wasn't Yellow Elk."

"So say I," answered Rasco. "But we'll git him yet, mark my words!"

With all possible speed they ran out of the cave and to the spot where they had left their horses. Here a disagreeable surprise awaited them. Every animal was gone, including the one Pawnee Brown had ridden.

"More of Yellow Elk's work!" muttered the boomer. "I'll tell you, men, that red is a corker, and as a dead Indian he couldn't be beat."

"I declar' this most stumps me!" growled Dan Gilbert. "Here's the trail plain enough, but it's all out of the question ter follow on shank's own mare."

"Let us hunt up Clemmer and the others," suggested Jack Rasco.

"We must be cautious--the cavalry may be somewhere in the vicinity," added Pawnee Brown. "How the redskins escaped them is a mystery to me."

"They are evidently as sly as their forefathers," said Dick. "But, really, something ought to be done. If we--hullo, there's a horse down in yonder clearing!"

"Bonnie Bird!" shouted Pawnee Brown, in great delight. It was indeed the beautiful mare. A second cry and the steed came bounding up to her master.

"Now I can follow even if the others can't," said the scout. "Rasco, it's a pity you haven't a mount. It is no more than right that you should follow up your niece. If you insist upon it I'll let you have Bonnie Bird. I wonder if Nellie or the redskin had her?"

"I won't take yer horse, Pawnee--it's askin' too much," answered Rasco. "Supposin' we both mount her? If Bonnie Bird got away from Yellow Elk it's more'n likely one of the other hosses got away, too."

"That's so. Well, get up, Jack, and let us lose no time."

Soon both men were mounted. A few words all around followed, and it was agreed that Dick and Gilbert should try to hunt up Clemmer and the others, and then away went Pawnee Brown and Rasco upon Yellow Elk's trail.

Suddenly Jack Rasco uttered a cry.

"See, Pawnee, here's whar another of the hosses got away. Hang me if I don't think it war my hoss, too!"

"Yes, and here is where the horse dropped into a walk," he answered. "I don't believe he can be far off."

Without delay Rasco slid to the ground.

"I'll follow him up afoot," he declared. "I'm fresh and can run it putty good. You go ahead with the regular trail."

The trail left by Yellow Elk ran down along the edge of the stream for a distance of perhaps a hundred yards, then it came out on a series of flat rocks and was lost to view.

Pawnee Brown came to a halt. Had Yellow Elk crossed the stream, or doubled on the trail and gone back?

Dismounting, he got down upon his hands and knees and examined the last hoof-prints with extreme care.

The examination lasted for fully ten minutes. No white man could follow a trail better than this leader of the boomers, yet for the time being he was baffled.

Yellow Elk had led the horses into the water, but the trail did not extend across the stream.

"He's an artful dodger!" mused Pawnee Brown, when of a sudden he became silent.

A faint scratching, as of tree bark, had come to his ears. The noise was but a short distance away.

"Some animal," he thought. "No human being would make such a sound as that."

Another ten seconds of painful silence followed. The scratching sound had just been resumed when Bonnie Bird wheeled about as if on a pivot.

"Ha!"

The exclamation came from between Pawnee Brown's set teeth. There, from between the branches of a tree just in front of him, glared a pair of yellowish-green eyes.

The blazing optics belonged to a monstrous wildcat!

As quick as a flash Pawnee Brown raised his pistol and pulled the trigger.

Crack! The wildcat was hit in the side. The shot was a glancing one and did but little damage.

Whirr! down came the body straight for the boomer, landing half upon his shoulder and half upon Bonnie Bird's mane.

The little mare was thoroughly frightened, and giving a snort and a plunge she threw both rider and wildcat to the ground.

As Pawnee Brown went down he tried to push the monstrous cat from him, but the beast had its claws fastened in the scout's clothing and could not be shook off.

Crack! Again Pawnee Brown fired. The flash was almost directly in the wildcat's face, and shot in the left forepaw the beast uttered a fearful howl of pain and dropped back.

But only for an instant. The pain only increased its anger, and with gleaming teeth it crouched down and made another spring, right for the boomer's throat.

Crack! crack! twice again the pistol rang out. But the big cat was now wary and both shots failed to take effect.

The pistol being now empty, Pawnee Brown hurled it at the enraged beast, striking it in the nose and eliciting another scream of rage.

Then, as the wildcat came on for a final attack, the scout pulled out his hunting knife.

As the wildcat came down the hand holding the hunting knife was raised, with the blade of the knife pointing upward.

A lightning-like swing and a thrust, and for one brief instant the wildcat was poised in the air, upon the very blade of the long knife.

The blow had been a true one, the knife point reaching the beast's heart, and when the animal fell it rolled down among the leaves, dead.

"By thunder! but that was something I hadn't bargained for!" murmured the great scout, as he surveyed the carcass. "That's about the biggest wildcat I ever saw. It's a good thing I didn't meet him in the dark."

Wiping off his hunting knife, he restored it to his belt. Then he picked up his pistol and started to reload it, at the same time whistling for Bonnie Bird, who, he felt sure, must be close by.

As Pawnee Brown stood reloading the pistol and whistling for his mare he did not notice a shadow behind him. Slowly but surely someone was drawing closer to him. It was Yellow Elk.

The Indian chief was on foot. In his left hand he carried a cocked revolver, in his right an old-time tomahawk, from which he had refused to be parted when placed on the Indian reservation.

The redskin's face was full of the most bitter animosity it is possible to imagine. The glare of wickedness in his eyes fairly put the look that had lived in the wildcat's optics to shame. His snags of yellow teeth were firmly set.

He was resolved to kill his enemy there and then. Pawnee Brown should not again escape him.

CHAPTER XVII.
THE MEETING IN THE WOODS.

After leaving Pawnee Brown, Jack Rasco followed the trail of his horse through a small grove of trees and along the upper bank of the very stream upon which the great scout encountered Yellow Elk.

"Blamed ef he didn't go further nor I expected," muttered Rasco to himself as he trudged along. But the hoof-prints were now growing fresher and fresher, telling that the animal could not be far off.

The woods passed, he began ascending a small hill. At the top of this was a level patch, thickly overgrown with short brush.

He had just entered the brush when he heard a strange sound. He listened intently.

"Thet's a hoss in pain," he said to himself. "Too bad if the critter hez had a tumble an' broke a leg! If that's---- By gum!"

Jack had stumbled upon a large opening directly in the midst of the brush. Before he could turn back the very soil beneath his feet gave way, and over and over he rolled down an incline of forty-five degrees, to bring up at last at the edge of a pool of black water and mud.

Fortunately he was not hurt, although the roll had dazed him and cut short his wind. As soon as he could he leaped to his feet and gazed around him.

The horse he had heard lay half in and half out of the mud. Its leg was caught between two rocks, and it was trying frantically to free itself. It was his own beast, and at once recognized him.

"Whoa there!" cried Rasco, and did all he could to soothe the animal. The horse appeared to understand that assistance was at hand, and became quiet, while Rasco quickly released the locked leg and the beast floundered up to a safe footing.

"Well, we're in a pocket, 'pears ter me," reflected the man of the plains as he gazed about him. On three sides the walls of the hole were very nearly perpendicular, on the fourth the slant was as previously stated, but here the soil was spongy and treacherous.

"Hang me ef I'm a-goin' ter stay here all day," muttered Rasco, after a view of the situation. "Come, boy, it's up thet slope or nuthin'," and he leaped on the horse's back and urged him forward on a run.

Twice did the horse try to ascend to the plain above and fail. Then Rasco urged him forward a third time. This time the beast balked and away went the man of the plains over his head.

Fortunately Rasco landed in a tolerably soft spot, otherwise his neck would surely have been broken. As it was, his head struck the root of a fallen tree, which had once stood upon the edge of the hole, and he rolled back near the pool all but senseless.

It was a quarter of an hour later before he felt like stirring again.

"Hang the hoss!" he murmured half aloud, yet, all told, he did not blame the animal so much for balking. "Couldn't do it, eh, boy?" he said, and the beast shook his mane knowingly.

"Git along alone, then!" went on Rasco, and struck the horse on the flank.

Away went the steed, and this time the top of the hole was gained without much difficulty.

"Now you're out, how am I ter make it?"

It was easy to ask this question, but not so easy to answer it. Rasco tried to run up the spongy incline and sank to his knees.

"Ain't no use; I'll try a new game," he growled.

Fortunately, Rasco was in the habit of carrying, in cowboy fashion, a lariat suspended from his belt. This he now unwound and with a dexterous throw caught the outer loop over a sturdy bush growing over one of the perpendicular sides of the opening.

Testing the lariat, to make certain it was firm, he began to ascend hand over hand. This was no light task, yet it was speedily accomplished, and with a sigh of relief he found himself safe once more.

But in the meantime the horse had trotted off, alarmed by a black snake in the long grass. Rasco saw this snake a minute later, but the reptile slunk out of sight before he could get a chance to dispatch it.

The trail of the horse led again back to the ravine, but not in the direction of the cave. Bound to secure the animal before rejoining Pawnee Brown, Rasco loped along in pursuit.

He was in the ravine, and had just caught sight of his steed once more, when he heard several pistol shots coming from a distance. These were the shots fired by Pawnee Brown at the wildcat. He listened intently, but no more shots followed, and being below the level of the surrounding country, he was unable to locate the discharge of firearms.

"Something is wrong somewhar," he mused. "Can thet be Pawnee shootin', or is it Dick an' the others?"

He secured the horse and began to ascend out of the ravine, when a murmur of voices broke upon his ears. One of the voices sounded familiar and he soon recognized it as that of Louis Vorlange.

Instantly dismounting, he tied his animal fast to a tree that the creature might not wander away again, and worked his way noiselessly through the brush. The voices came from a nearby clearing, and approaching, Rasco saw on horseback Louis Vorlange and half a dozen cavalrymen, among them Tucker, Ross and Skimmy, the trio who had sought to detain Dick as a horse thief.

"I feel certain they will come this way," one of the strange troopers was saying. "I saw at least two boomer spies along yonder ravine."

"They will come to Honnewell," answered Vorlange. "It may be that instead of making a rush they will try to sneak in during the night, one at a time."

"We'll be ready for 'em," muttered Tucker. "I know my meat," he added, significantly, to Vorlange, meaning that he had not forgotten the reward offered if, in a battle he should lay Pawnee Brown and Dick low. At the words Vorlange nodded.

"When will the reinforcements be up this way?" asked Ross.

"I have already sent word to headquarters," answered Vorlange. "The lieutenant is sure to respond without delay."

"Do you reckon the boomers know we are on hand to stop them?" questioned Skimmy.

"They know nothing," answered Vorlange. "If Pawnee Brown leads his men in this direction they will fall directly into a trap--if the lieutenant does as I have advised, and I think he will."

"I hope the boomers start to fight and give us a chance to wipe 'em out," muttered Ross.

"There will be a fight started, don't you fear," answered Vorlange.

The spy meant what he said. Too cowardly to meet Pawnee Brown face to face, he wanted to make sure that the great scout should be killed.

This would happen if a battle came off, for he felt sure Tucker would do exactly as he promised.

Vorlange had determined to be on hand. Secreted in a tree or elsewhere he could fire a dozen shots or so into the air, and this would arouse both cavalrymen and boomers to think that actual hostilities had already started, and then neither side would longer hold off.

"When will the boomers move?" was one of the cavalryman's questions.

"They are waiting for Pawnee Brown," said the spy.

"Where is he?"

"Somewhere about the country."

"Can he be up here?"

Vorlange started.

"I--I think not.

"He's a slick one, Vorlange; remember that."

"I know it, but some men are slicker. Wait until this boom is busted and you'll never hear of Pawnee Brown again."

So the talk ran on. Rasco listened with much interest, forgetting the fact that he had promised to follow Pawnee Brown as soon as the stray-away horse was secured.

What he had heard surprised him greatly.

Many of the plans of the boomers, made in such secrecy, were known to the government authorities. The plan to move westward to Honnewell was known, and a passage through to Oklahoma from that direction was, consequently, out of the question.

"The boys must know of this," thought Rasco. "I must tell Clemmer and Gilbert before I try to hunt up Pawnee again, or go after Nellie. If there was a fight as Vorlange seems to think, there might be a hundred or more killed."

Having overheard all that he deemed necessary, the man of the plains started to retreat.

He had taken but a few steps when he found himself cut off from his horse.

Three additional cavalrymen were approaching from the thicket.

"Here's a horse tied up!" cried one. "Boys, whose animal is this?"

The call instantly attracted the attention of Vorlange and his companions. They turned toward the speaker, and now there remained nothing for Rasco to do but to run for it, and this he did at the top of his speed.

As long as he could he kept out of sight behind the bushes. But soon Tucker caught sight of him.

"Halt, or I'll fire!" came the command.

Tucker spoke first, and several others followed. As Rasco was now in plain view, and as each of the enemy had a firearm of some sort aimed at him, it would have been foolishness to have thus courted death, and the man of the plains halted.

"It is Jack Rasco!" cried Vorlange. "Boys, this is Pawnee Brown's right-hand man!"

"I know him!" growled Tucker. "Rasco, you're in a box now and don't you forget it. You've been spying on us."

"Make him a prisoner," said another of the cavalrymen, an under officer. "If he is a spy we'll have to take him back to the fort and turn him over to the captain."

A minute later Jack Rasco found himself a close prisoner. It was destined to be some time ere he again obtained his liberty. Thus were his chances of helping Pawnee Brown cut off.

CHAPTER XVIII.
A CRY FROM THE DARKNESS.

Let us return to Pawnee Brown, who, totally unconscious of the fact that Yellow Elk was creeping up behind him, stood beside the body of the dead wildcat, re-loading the empty revolver.

One of the chambers of the firearm had been loaded, when something about the pistol caused the great scout to examine it more closely. As he was doing this Yellow Elk advanced to within three feet of him and raised the tomahawk for the fatal blow.

At this terrible moment it must surely have been Providence which interfered in the boomer's behalf, for, totally unconscious of his peril, he would have done absolutely nothing to save himself. He bent over the pistol more closely.

"That trigger seems to catch," he thought, and threw the weapon up and fired it over his shoulder, just to test it.

The bullet did not pass within a yard of Yellow Elk, but the movement came so unexpectedly that the Indian chief was taken completely off his guard and dropped back as though actually shot. His cry of astonishment and fear lasted longer than did the pistol report, and Pawnee Brown swung around to confront him.

"Yellow Elk!" came from his lips, when whizz! the tomahawk left the redskin's hand and came swirling through the air directly for his head. He dropped like lightning, and the keen blade sank deeply into the tree behind him.

"Wough!" grunted the Indian when he saw how he had missed his mark. Then he leveled the pistol in his left hand at Pawnee Brown's head.

The great scout felt his position was still a trying one. His own shooter, though still in hand, was empty. He pointed it and started to back away to the tree behind him.

"Stop, or I kill!" commanded Yellow Elk, but instead of complying, the scout took a flying leap to a safe shelter. Seeing this, Yellow Elk also lost no time in getting behind cover.

With the pistol loaded once more the boomer felt safer. He listened intently for some movement upon the part of his enemy, but none came. The Indian is a great hand at playing a waiting game and Yellow Elk was no exception to this rule.

"Well, if you can wait, so can I," thought Pawnee Brown and settled down with eyes and ears on the alert. He thought of Nellie Winthrop and of Rasco, and wondered what had become of uncle and niece. He did not want to wait, feeling it was important to get back to the boomers' camp, but there was no help for it, and he remained where he was.

Fifteen minutes went by and no sound broke the stillness saving that of the water in the brook as it flowed down over a series of rocks. Then came the faint crack of a single dry twig over upon his left. He turned around and blazed away in that direction.

A fierce but suppressed exclamation in the Indian tongue followed, showing that Yellow Elk had been hit. How serious the Indian chief was injured there was no telling. It might be only a flesh wound, it might have been fatal and Yellow Elk might have died without further sound, and then again it might be only a ruse. Again Pawnee Brown paused to listen.

Thus another quarter of an hour was wasted. It must be confessed that the great scout's nerves were strung to the topmost tension. At any moment a shot might come which would end his life. It was ten times more trying than to stand up in line of battle, for the enemy could not be seen.

Again came the crack of a twig, but very faint, showing that the sound came from a distance. There followed a faint splash, some distance up the stream. Yellow Elk was retreating.

"I reckon I hit him pretty bad," mused Pawnee Brown. "But I'll go slow--it may be only a trick," and away he crawled as silently as a snail along the brook's bank.

Inside of the next half hour he had covered a territory of many yards on both sides of the brook. In one spot he had seen several drops of blood and the finger marks of a bloody hand. Yellow Elk, however, had completely disappeared.

"He is gone, and so is the trail," muttered the great scout at last. He spoke the truth. Further following of the Indian chief was just then out of the question.

"There is one thing to be thankful for," he mused. "I don't believe he captured Nellie Winthrop again after he left the cave. I wonder what has become of that girl?"

Bonnie Bird had wandered down the brook for a drink and instantly returned at her master's call. With something of a sigh at not having finished matters with Yellow Elk the boomer leaped once again into the saddle and turned back in the direction from whence he had come.

It was now growing dark, and the great scout felt that he must ere long return to the boomers' camp and give the order necessary to start the long wagon train on its way westward to Honnewell. Little did he dream of what the government spy and the cavalrymen had discovered and how Jack Rasco had been taken prisoner.

"Pawnee!"

It was a cry from a patch of woods to the northward, and straining his eyes he saw Cal Clemmer waving his sombrero toward him. Scout and cowboy boomer were soon together.

"Well, whar's Rasco and the gal?" were Clemmer's first words.

"Both gone--I don't know where, Cal. Where are the other boys?"

"Started back toward Honnewell; thet is, all but Dick Arbuckle. He's over ter yonder spring gittin' a drink o' water."

"I am sorry I failed to find the girl," said Pawnee Brown. "She must have wandered off in the woods and got lost. I am quite certain the Indians did not spot her again."

"And Jack?"

"Went off after his horse."

"Wot do yer advise us ter do--stay here?"

"I am afraid staying here will do no good, Cal. I must get back to camp and start the wagons up. I know they won't move a step unless I am personally there to give directions. The old boomers are all afraid of being fooled by some trick of the soldiers."

"Thet's so. Wall, if yer want me ter stay here I'll stay--otherwise I'll go back," concluded Clemmer.

Dick now came up, as anxious as Clemmer had been to know the news. His face grew very sober when he heard that Nellie had not been found.

"I wish I knew more of this territory--I'd go after her myself," he said, earnestly. "I hope you won't abandon the search?"

"Oh, no, lad; that is not my style. But I must get back to the camp first and start the train along. I'll be on this ground again by midnight."

"Then why can't I stay here? I am not afraid."

"Alone?" ejaculated Clemmer.

"Yes--if you want to join Pawnee."

"By gosh, but that boy's nervy fer a city chap!" cried the cowboy boomer, in admiration.

"Well, you know there's a girl in this, Cal," rejoined Pawnee Brown, dryly. "And I reckon she's a girl well worth going through fire and water for."

At this Dick blushed.

"I want to find out about Rasco, too," he hastened to say. "You know I was going through with him, and he was going to do some business for my father, later on."

The matter was talked over for several minutes, and it was at last decided that Dick should secrete himself in a thicket and stand watch there or close by until he heard from Pawnee Brown again.

"Be on your guard, boy, for enemies may be thick here," were the boomer's last words of caution. "Don't uncover to anybody until you are positive it is a friend."

"And here's a bite for yer," added Clemmer, handing out some rations he carried in a haversack. "You'll get mighty hungry ere the sun comes up again."

In a minute more the two horsemen were galloping away. Dick watched them until they were lost to view, then dropped to a sitting position on a flat rock in the centre of a clump of trees.

The youth's heart beat rather strongly. He was not used to this sort of thing. How different the prairies and woods were to the city streets and buildings.

"Lonesome isn't a name for it," he mused. "Puts me in mind of one vast cemetery--a gigantic Greenwood, only there aren't any monuments. What is that?"

There was a flutter and a whirl, and Dick grasped his pistol tighter. It was only a night-bird, starting up now that the sun was beginning to set.

Soon the woods and the prairies began to grow dark. The sun was lost to view behind tall trees which cast shadows of incalculable length. It grew colder, too, and he buttoned his light coat tightly about him.

To pass the time he began to eat some of the food left behind by Clemmer. It was not particularly appetizing, and in the city Dick might have passed it by for something better. But just then it tasted "just boss," to use Dick's own words. A bracing air and hunger are the best sauces in the world.

An hour had gone by, and all was dark, when Dick started up from a reverie into which he had fallen. What was that which had reached his ears from a distance? Was it a cry, or merely the moaning of the rising wind?

He listened. No, it was not the wind--it was a cry--a girl's voice--the voice of Nellie Winthrop!

"It is Nellie!" came from his set lips, and his face grew pale. Again came the cry, but this time more faintly.

From what direction had that cry for help proceeded? In vain the boy asked himself that question. He was not used to a life in the open and the rising wind was very deceptive.

"I must find her!" he gasped, leaping from the rocks. "I shan't remain here while she is in trouble."

He had no horse the men being unable to provide him with one when they had come together, but for this he did not care. He was resolved to aid the girl if such a thing were possible.

Away he went over the prairie at a rapid gait, in the direction from whence he imagined the cry had proceeded. Two hundred yards were covered and he came to a halt and listened. Not a sound broke the stillness, although he fancied he heard the hoof-strokes of a horse at a great distance.

Then he turned in another direction, and then another. It was all to no purpose. No trace of the girl could be found. He gave a groan.

"It's no use; she's gone and that is all there is to it. Poor girl!"

With a sinking heart he set off to return to the spot from whence he had come. He advanced a dozen steps, then halted and stared about him.

Suddenly an awful truth burst upon him. He was lost among the brush!

CHAPTER XIX.
NELLIE MEETS VORLANGE.

What had that awful cry heard by Dick meant?

To learn the particulars, we must go back to the time when Nellie Winthrop started to escape from the cave in the cliff.

The heart of the poor girl almost stopped beating as she saw Pawnee Brown face about, ready to defend both her and himself from any enemy who might appear to help Yellow Elk.

Urged by the great scout, she set off on a hasty run for the mouth of the cave.

Before the entrance was gained she heard the crack of a pistol, but whether fired by the boomer or an Indian she could not tell.

"Heaven spare that brave man!" was the prayer which came to her almost bloodless lips.

She looked around in vain for the horse spoken of by Pawnee Brown. Not an animal was in sight. Then she remembered what the scout had said about riding down the ravine, and she set off on foot.

Not far from the mouth of the cave the ravine forked into two branches, the smaller fork ending at the distance of quarter of a mile in a cul de sac, or blind pocket. Not knowing she was making any mistake, she entered this fork and kept on running, expecting each instant to find Pawnee Brown coming up behind her.

"Oh, dear, I can't be right!"

Such was the cry which escaped her when she came to a halt, realizing she could go no further in that direction. On both sides and in front arose a series of rocks, more or less steep, and covered only with scrub brush, impossible to ascend.

She looked behind. No one was coming. All about her was as silent as a tomb.

"Perhaps I had better go back," she mused, but the thought of encountering an

Indian made her shiver. In her life in the open she had had many an encounter with a wild animal, but redskins were as yet almost new to her, and her experience with the hideous Yellow Elk had been one she did not care to repeat.

She had just turned to move back to the ravine proper, when a sound among the rocks caused her to pause. She looked intently in the direction, but could see nothing out of the ordinary.

"Hullo, there, miss; what are you doing away out here?"

The cry came from the rocks on her right. Turning swiftly, she saw an evil-looking man scowling down upon her from a small opening under one of the rocky walls of the *cul de sac*. The man was Louis Vorlange.

Nellie did not know the fellow; indeed she had never heard of him. But there was that in the spy's manner which was not at all reassuring as he leaped down to where she stood.

"I say, how did you come here?" went on Vorlange.

"I--I just escaped from an Indian who carried me off from Arkansas City," answered Nellie.

"An Indian! Who was it, do you know?"

"A fellow named Yellow Elk."

Vorlange uttered a low whistle.

"Where is he now?" he questioned.

"I left him back in yonder hills, in a cave."

Again the spy uttered a whistle, but whether of surprise or dismay Nellie could not tell.

"Were you alone with Yellow Elk?"

"I was for a time. But a white man came to my aid and the two had a fight."

"Who was the white man?"

Before she gave the matter a second thought, Nellie answered:

"Mr. Pawnee Brown."

"Ha!" Vorlange's eyes gleamed, and the girl felt certain she had made a mistake.

"Where is Pawnee Brown now?"

"I left him in the cave with the Indian. I expected him to follow me."

"I see. And what may your name be?"

The man's words were fair enough, but Nellie did not like his manner at all, so she turned upon him coldly.

"And what is your name, and who are you?"

"I am not here to answer questions, miss. I am a government official, let that be enough for you to know."

As he spoke Louis Vorlange caught Nellie by the arm.

"Let go of me," cried the frightened girl, and attempted to pull away, but Vorlange held her tight.

"You come along with me. No one, and especially Pawnee Brown, has any right in this territory just now, and it is my business to see that all such people are kept out. I presume you belong to that crowd of boomers, since you say you were carried off from Arkansas City?"

"I shall answer no more of your questions, sir. Let me go!"

"You'll come along with me," muttered Vorlange. "I take it you know what the boomers intend to do, and, if that is so, your information is just what the government wants."

So speaking he attempted to drag Nellie up the rocks to the opening before mentioned. The girl resisted with all of her strength, and Vorlange received a box on the left ear which made that member of his body hum for a long time after.

"You little wretch!" he cried, as he caught her up in his arms. "I will get square with you for that."

"You are no gentleman! Let me go!" replied Nellie. Then she attempted to scream, but he promptly clapped his hand over her mouth.

In another moment, despite her utmost struggles, he was carrying her up to the opening. This spot once reached, he took her inside and over to a well-like hole upon one side.

"Do you see that hole?" he said sternly. "I am going to put you in that for the present, for safe keeping. I call it my prison cell, and no cell could be better. It is not a cheerful place, but you will be as safe there as in the best prison in Chicago or San Francisco. I'll be back for you soon, and in the meantime you had better make no attempt to escape, for at the mouth of this opening is set a gun, with a wire attachment, which may blow you up."

This latter statement was a false one, but Vorlange rightfully calculated that it would have its due effect upon the frightened girl.

Having thus intimidated Nellie, Vorlange lowered her into the opening in the rocks, which was about six feet in diameter and at least ten feet deep. This done, he lit a lantern and hung it so that its rays might shine down upon his captive.

"You won't feel so lonesome with the light," he said. "Now keep quiet until I return. If you behave yourself you have nothing to fear. I am a government officer and I am holding you as a prisoner only until I can turn you over to the proper authorities."

"It is a--a queer proceeding," faltered Nellie. She could hardly bring herself to believe the man.

"Out here we can't do things exactly as they are done in the big cities," grinned Vorlange. "We are out here after the boomers just now, and your being here with Pawnee Brown will rather go against you. But keep quiet now until I return."

Thus speaking, the spy quirted the opening, leaving Nellie alone. With hasty steps Vorlange made his way along the fork of the ravine until the opening proper was reached. Here he settled himself in a tree to watch for Pawnee Brown's possible coming. But, as we know, the scout did not move in that direction.

For over two hours Nellie was left alone, a prey to the keenest mental torture it is possible to imagine. As the day was drawing to a close Vorlange appeared, a peculiar smile upon his face.

He had met the cavalrymen, and Jack Rasco had been captured as previously described.

"Well, we are going to move now," he said to Nellie, and threw down a rope that he might haul her up out of the hole.

"Where to?"

"You'll learn that later."

As she did not wish to remain in that damp spot longer, she caught the rope and was drawn up. Then Vorlange took her outside and sat her down before him on his horse, first, however, tying her hands.

It was during the ride that followed that Dick heard her cry for help and started to her rescue, only to miss her and get lost in the brush.

A ride of half an hour brought the pair to the edge of a heavy timber. Through this they picked their way, until a small clearing was gained, where was located a low log cabin, containing two rooms. The log cabin was not inhabited, and Vorlange pushed open the door without ceremony.

"You'll stay here over night," he said, as he ushered Nellie into the smaller room. "You can see this has been used for a prison before, as all of the windows are nailed up. I don't believe you'll try to escape anyway, for, let me warn you, it won't pay. Make yourself as comfortable as you can, and in the morning we'll come to an understanding. We've got another prisoner besides yourself, and between the two of you I reckon we'll find out before long just what the boomers are up to."

And with a dark look upon his face, Louis Vorlange stalked out of the apartment, locking the door after him, and thus leaving Nellie to her fate.

CHAPTER XX.
THE MOVING OF THE BOOMERS.

P awnee Brown at last!"

The words came from one of the boomers, a fat but spry old chap named Dunbar.

"Yes, Dunbar," answered the great scout. "Were you getting anxious about me?"

"Well, just a trifle, Pawnee."

"The camp must move at once. Send the word around immediately, Dunbar."

"Whar do we move to?"

"To Honnewell. As soon as all hands are at Honnewell I'll send out further orders."

In less than half an hour the immense wagon train organized by the boomers located in Kansas was on the way.

At the front rode Pawnee Brown, Clemmer and several others who were personal friends of the scout.

It was a grand sight, this moving. To this day some of the boomers say it was the grandest sight they ever beheld.

Every heart was full of hope. Past trials and hardships were forgotten. The boomers were to enter the richest farming lands in the States and there start life anew.

The movement was made in silence and in almost utter darkness. Of course, it was impossible to hide the news from the citizens of Arkansas City, but the train was well on its way before the news had any chance of spreading.

At the time of which we write there were several trails to Honnewell from Arkansas City. The regular road was a fair one in good weather, but, after such a rain as had fallen, this trail was hub-deep with mud in more than one spot.

"Oi'll not go thot trail," was Delaney's comment. "Oi'll take the upper road."

"Thot's roight, Mike," put in Rosy, his wife. "It's not meself as wants to stick fast in this black mud. Sure, and it's worse nor the bogs of Erin!"

"Vot's dot road you vos speakin' apout alretty?" put in Humpendinck, who had as heavy a wagon as anyone.

"It's a better road nor this, Humpy," replied Mike Delaney. "Folly me an' we'll rach Honnewell afore enny of 'em, mark me wurrud."

Thus encouraged, Humpendinck followed Delaney on the upper trail, and, seeing the two go off, half a dozen followed.

It was more than half an hour after before Pawnee Brown heard of their departure.

The great scout was much disturbed.

"It's foolishness for them to start off on the upper trail," he declared. "I went over it but a few days ago, and at Brown's Crossing the road is all torn up by a freshet. Besides that, we must keep together."

"Yer right thar, Pawnee," answered Clemmer. "Delaney ought to know better. But yer can't tell the Irish anything."

"Humpendinck went with him," put in Dunbar, who had brought the news.

"Both the Irishman and the German are smart enough in their way," answered Pawnee Brown. "But they've made a mistake. Cal and Dunbar, you continue at the head, and I'll ride across country and head Delaney and his crowd back through the Allen trail. I'll probably rejoin you just this side of Honnewell."

With this command, Pawnee Brown left the wagon train and plunged off through the darkness alone.

He had been over that district many times and thought he knew about every foot of the ground.

But for once the great scout was mistaken, and that mistake was destined to bring him into serious difficulty.

About half a mile had been covered, and he was just approaching a patch of small timber, when he noticed that Bonnie Bird began to show signs of shyness. She did not refuse to go forward, but evidently was proceeding against her will.

Quick to notice a change in the beautiful mare's mood, Pawnee Brown spoke to her. She pawed the ground and tossed her head.

"What is it, Bonnie? Danger ahead?"

Again the mare pawed the ground. Feeling certain something was wrong, Pawnee Brown stood up in his stirrups and looked about him.

All was dark and silent upon every side. Overhead the faint stars shed but an uncertain light.

"It's one too many for me, Bonnie," he mused. "Forward until the danger becomes clearer."

Thus commanded, the mare moved forward once more, but this time much slower. Once or twice her feet seemed to stick fast, but Pawnee Brown did not notice this. At last she came to a dead halt and would not go another step.

"The danger must be in the timber," thought the boomer. "Bonnie Bird wouldn't balk for nothing. I'll dismount and reconnoitre."

Springing to the ground, he drew his pistol and moved forward silently. Scarcely had he taken a dozen steps than he realized the cause of his mare's unwillingness to proceed further.

He was in a bed of quicksand.

Anybody who knows what a bed of quicksand is knows how dangerous it is--dangerous to both man and beast. Just as the scout made his discovery he sank up to his knees in the mass.

"By Jove! I must get back out of this, and in double-quick order," he muttered, and tried to turn, to find himself sinking up to his waist.

Pawnee Brown was now fully alive to the grave peril of his situation.

He tried by all the strength at his command to pull himself to the firm ground from which he had started.

He could not budge a foot. True, he took one step, but it was only to sink in deeper than ever.

Several minutes of great anxiety passed. He had sunk very nearly up to his armpits.

Quarter of an hour more and he would be up to his head, and then----? Brave as he was, the great scout did not dare to think further. The idea of a death in the treacherous quicksand was truly horrible.

His friends would wonder what had become of him, but it was not likely that they would ever find his body.

And even faithful Bonnie Bird would be dumb, so far as telling the particulars of her master's disappearance was concerned.

The mare now stood upon the edge of the quicksands, fifteen feet off, whining anxiously. She knew as well as though she had been a human being that something was wrong.

Suddenly an inspiration came to Pawnee Brown.

"How foolish! Why didn't I think of that before?" he muttered.

At his belt had hung a lariat, placed there when the wagon train started, in case any of the animals should attempt to run off in the darkness.

The boomer could use a lariat as well as Clemmer or any of the cowboys. More than once, riding at full speed upon his mare, he had thrown the noose around any foot of a steer that was selected by those looking on.

He put his hand down to his waist and felt for the lariat. It was still there, and he brought it up and swung it over his head, to free it from the quicksand.

As has been stated, the belt of timber was not far away, the nearest tree being less than fifty feet from where he remained stuck.

Preparing the lariat, he threw the noose up and away from him. It circled through the air and fell over the nearest branch of the tree. Hauling it taut, Pawnee Brown tested it, to make sure it would not slip, and then began to haul himself up, as Rasco had done at the swamp hole.

It was slow work, and more than once he felt that the lariat would break, so great was the strain put upon it.

But it held, and a few minutes later Pawnee Brown found himself with somewhat cut hands, safe in the branches of the tree.

Winding up the lariat, he descended to the ground, and made a detour to where Bonnie Bird remained standing, and to where he had cast his pistol.

The mare and weapon secured, he continued on his way, but made certain to wander into no more quicksand spots.

"It was too narrow an escape for comfort," was the way in which Pawnee Brown expressed himself, when he told the story later.

An hour after found him again among the boomers.

Mike Delaney was just coming in by the Allen trail. The Irishman was much crestfallen over his failure to find a better trail than that selected by the scout, and Rosy was giving it to him with a vengeance.

"Th' nixt toime ye go forward it will be undher Pawnee Brown's directions, Moike Delaney!" she cried. "It's not yerself thot is as woise as Moses in the wilderness, moind thot!" And her clenched fist shook vigorously to emphasize her words. After that Delaney never strayed from the proper trail again.

All of the boomers but Jack Rasco were now on hand, and as hour after hour went by and Rasco did not turn up, Pawnee Brown grew anxious about the welfare of his right-hand man.

"Looking for the girl had brought him into trouble, more than likely," he thought, as he rode away from Honnewell, taking a due south course. "And what can have become of her?"

Pawnee Brown was on his way to the spot where he had left Dick. He had decided that as soon as he had found the lad, he would return to camp, and then the onward march of the boomers for Oklahoma should at once be begun.

On through the ravine where he had met Yellow Elk he dashed, Bonnie Bird feeling fresh after a short rest and her morning meal, for the sun was now creeping skyward. On through the brush, and he turned toward the open prairie.

"Halt! Throw up your hands!"

The unexpected command came from the thicket on the edge of the prairie. On the instant the boomer wheeled about. The sight which met his gaze caused his heart to sink within him. There, drawn up in line, was the full troop of cavalry sent out by the government to stop the boomers' entrance to the much-coveted territory.

Vorlange's spy work was responsible, and Pawnee Brown's carefully-laid plan had fallen through.

CHAPTER XXI.
DICK'S DISAGREEABLE DISCOVERY.

Lost!"

Dick murmured the word over and over again, as he peered through the brush, first in one direction and then in another.

"I ought to have kept track of where I was going," he went on bitterly. "Of course, away out here one place is about as good as another for hiding, but how am I going to find the others, or, rather, how are they going to find me, when they come back?"

He pushed on for nearly a quarter of an hour; then, coming to a flat rock, threw himself down for reflection.

"Just my luck!" he muttered. "I'll have to have a string tied about my neck like a poodle dog. What a clown I was to go it blind! But Nellie's cry for help made me forget everything else. Poor girl! I do hope she is safe. If that redskin--gosh! what's that?"

The flat rock was backed up by a number of heavy bushes. From these bushes had come a peculiar noise, half grunt, half yawn! Dick leaped to his feet, the bushes parted and there appeared the savage face of Yellow Elk!

Dick knew the Indian by that plume of which he had heard so much. He rightfully guessed that Yellow Elk had been taking a nap behind the bushes. He had been shot in the thigh, and this, coupled with the fact that he had had no sleep for two nights, had made him very weary.

As the Indian chief shoved his face into view he caught sight of Dick and uttered a slight huh! Up came the boy's weapon, but on the instant Yellow Elk disappeared.

For the moment Dick was too paralyzed to move. Like a flash he realized that

Yellow Elk had the better of him, for the Indian was behind shelter, while he stood in a clearing.

"White boy stand still!" came in guttural tones from the redskin. "Don't dare move, or Indian shoot."

"What do you want of me?" asked Dick.

"White boy all alone?"

"What business is that of yours?"

At this Yellow Elk muttered a grunt. Then from out of the bushes Dick saw thrust the shining barrel of a horse pistol.

"White boy throw down little shooter," commanded the redskin. By little shooter he meant Dick's pistol.

There was no help for it, and the youth did as requested.

"White boy got udder shooter?"

"No."

"Now say if white boy alone. Speak if want to save life."

"Yes, I am alone, Yellow Elk."

"Ha! you know Yellow Elk?" cried the Indian in surprise.

"I've heard of you."

"What white boy do here?"

"I am lost."

"Lost. Huh!" and a look of disgust crossed the Indian chiefs face. The idea of a human being losing his way was something he could not understand. During his life he had covered thousands of miles of prairie and forest lands and had never yet lost himself. Such is the training and instinct of a true American aboriginal.

While speaking Yellow Elk had leaped through the brush, and now he came up and peered into Dick's face. Instantly his eyes filled with anger.

"I know white boy; he friend to Pawnee Brown. Indian see him at big moving."--meaning the camp of the boomers. He had not noticed Dick in the fight at the cave.

"Yes, Pawnee Brown is my friend," answered Dick. "Where is he now?" he added, to throw the Indian off the series of questions he was propounding.

"Pawnee Brown dead!" muttered Yellow Elk simply. "White boy come with me."

"With you!" ejaculated Dick, a chill creeping up to his heart.

"Yes; come now. No wait, or Yellow Elk shoot!" and again the horse pistol was raised.

The tone was so ugly that Dick felt it would be useless to hang back. Yellow Elk pointed with his arm in the direction he wished the lad to proceed, and away they went, the Indian but a pace behind, and keeping his pistol where it would be ready for use whenever required.

Dick never forgot that walk in the starlight, taken at about the same time that Pawnee Brown was floundering in the quicksand. A mile or more was covered, over prairies, through a wood and across several small streams, for the fertile Indian Territory abounds in water courses. Yellow Elk stuck to him like a shadow, and the pistol was continually in evidence. Yellow Elk had likewise appropriated Dick's weapon, the one cast to the ground.

Presently a clearing was gained where stood a cabin built of logs. All about the place was deserted. Going up to the cabin the Indian opened the door and lit a match.

"White boy go inside and we have talk," said Yellow Elk, when there came a noise from the woods beyond. At once Yellow Elk pushed Dick into the cabin and bolted the door from the outside.

"White boy keep quiet or Yellow Elk come in and kill!" he hissed, in a low but distinct tone. "No make a sound till Indian open door again."

The Indian's words were so terrifying that Dick stood still for several minutes exactly where he had been thrust. All was pitch dark around him. He listened, but not a sound reached his ears.

"Where in the world is this adventure going to end?" was the thought which coursed through his mind.

He wondered what had alarmed Yellow Elk. Was it the approach of some white friend? Fervidly he prayed it might be.

A low, half-suppressed cough from somewhere close at hand caught his ear and made him start.

"Who is there?" he asked aloud.

"Oh, Dick Arbuckle, is that you?" came in an eager voice.

"Nellie Winthrop! Is it possible? Where are you?"

"In the next room."

"Can't you come out?"

"No; I'm locked in."

"Gosh, you don't say!" Forgetting his former fear, Dick hurried across the cabin floor to the door of the inner apartment. Feeling around in the dark he found a hasp and staple and pulled out the plug which fastened the barrier. In another instant boy and girl plumped into each other's arms in the darkness. Even in that moment of peril Dick could not resist giving Nellie a little squeeze, which she did not resent.

"But how came you here?" asked the youth quickly.

"I was captured by a government spy, who wants to get from me some secret of the boomers. He is a bad-looking man, and I was awfully afraid of him."

"Yellow Elk brought me here. We are prisoners together. Some noise in the woods just took Yellow Elk off."

"The man has been gone less than five minutes. Perhaps they are in league with each other," suggested Nellie.

"Perhaps, or they may be enemies. But never mind how that stands. We must get away, Nellie, and that before Yellow Elk comes back."

"Heaven knows, I am willing!" gasped the trembling girl. "I want no more of Yellow Elk."

"The window is nailed up," went on Dick, after an examination. "And the Indian fastened that door from the outside. I wonder if I can't get out by way of the roof?" He lit a match and gazed upward. "There is an opening. Here goes!"

In another instant he was climbing up beside the fireplace, to where a scuttle led to the sloping roof. He was soon without, and Nellie heard him drop to the ground. Then the outer door was thrown back.

"Quick! The Indian is coming back, and there is somebody with him!" whispered Dick, and, taking hold of Nellie's hand, he led her away as fast as possible. Their course was from the rear of the cabin and across a broad but shallow stream.

"We'll go down the stream a bit before we land," said Dick, as they were on the point of stepping out of the water. "That may serve to throw Yellow Elk off the trail."

"Yes, yes, but do hurry!" answered the girl. "If Yellow Elk gets hold of me again I'll die!" The fear of getting into the clutches of the red man was so great she trembled from head to foot and would have gone down had not Dick's strong arm supported her.

It was wonderful how strong the youth felt, now that he had somebody besides himself to protect. It is said that nature fits the back to the burden, and it must have been so in this case. For himself, he might have feared to face Yellow Elk single-handed; defending Nellie he would, if called upon, have faced a dozen redskins.

On and on they went, as silently as possible. The trees overhung the brook from both sides, making it pitch dark beneath.

A distance of fifty yards had been covered, when they heard a loud exclamation of rage, followed by an Indian grunt.

"The white man and the Indian have met and both have discovered our flight," whispered Dick. "Come, we will leave the stream and take to yonder woods. Surely among those trees we can find some safe hiding place."

They turned in toward shore. As they were about to step to dry land Nellie's foot slipped on a round stone, making a loud splash. At the same time the girl gave a faint cry.

"My ankle--it's twisted!"

"Quick! let me carry you!" returned Dick, and, seeing the ankle must pain her not a little, he picked her up in his arms and dove in among the trees.

They were not a moment too soon, for the ready ears of Yellow Elk had heard the splash and the cry, and now he came bounding in the direction, with Louis Vorlange at his heels.

CHAPTER XXII.
DICK HITS HIS MARK.

They are coming closer, Dick! What shall we do?"

It was Nellie Winthrop who asked the question. Boy and girl had entered the woods a distance of fifty feet from the bank of the brook, and both rested where several large rocks and some overhanging bushes afforded a convenient hiding place.

"Keep quiet, Nellie," he said in a murmur, with his lips close to her shell-like ears. And he gripped her arm to show her that he would stand by her no matter what danger might befall them.

It would have been foolhardy to say more, for Yellow Elk and Louis Vorlange were now within hearing distance, and the ears of the Indian chief were more than ever on the alert. The government spy had lighted a torch, which he swung low to the brook bank, while Yellow Elk made an examination of the ground.

"Here footmarks!" grunted the redskin, a minute later, and pointed them out. "They go this way--cannot be far off."

"Then after them," muttered Vorlange. "It was through your stupidity that the girl got away. Yellow Elk, I always put you down for being smarter than that."

"Yellow Elk smart enough!" growled the Indian chief.

"No, you're not. In some things you are like a block of wood," grumbled Vorlange. The escape of Nellie had put him out a good deal.

The manner of the government spy provoked the Indian. To be called a block of wood is, to the red man, a direct insult. Yellow Elk straightened up.

"White man big fool!" he hissed. "Yellow Elk not make chase for him," and he folded his arms.

"You won't go after the boy and the girl?" queried Vorlange.

"No--white man hunt for himself if he want to catch the little woman again."

And having thus delivered himself, Yellow Elk sat down by the brook and refused to budge another step.

The Indian's objections to continuing the search were more numerous than appeared on the surface. The so-called insult, bad as it was, was merely an excuse to hide other motives. Yellow Elk had known Vorlange for years and as the spy was naturally a mean fellow, the redskin hated him accordingly.

Another reason for refusing to go ahead was that Yellow Elk knew only too well that if Dick and Nellie were again taken, Vorlange would consider both his own captives, and Yellow Elk would be "counted out" of the entire proceedings. He could not go to the agency and claim any glory, for he had run away without permission, although he had told Vorlange he was away on a special mission connected with the soldiers.

And deeper than all was the thought that if he did not capture Nellie now, he might do so later on, when he had separated from the spy. Ever since he had first seen the beautiful girl he had been covetous of making her his squaw. Indian fashion, he felt he could compel Nellie to choose him, even if he had to whip her into making the choice.

"You won't go on with the search?" cried Vorlange, in a rage.

"No," was the short answer.

"I say you shall! See here, Yellow Elk, do you want to be shot?"

"Yellow Elk not afraid of Vorlange--Vorlange know dat. Yellow Elk go back to cabin to see if girl or boy leave anything behind."

Then he got up, waded across the brook again and disappeared among the trees surrounding the log cabin.

Louis Vorlange muttered a good many things in a very angry tone. Then, torch in hand, he started up the brook bank to follow the trail alone.

Dick and Nellie listened to the quarrel with bated breath. Both hoped that Vorlange would follow to the cabin. When he approached closer than ever, their hearts seemed to almost stop beating.

Feeling that a contest was at hand, Dick groped around in the darkness for some weapon. No stick was at hand, but at his feet lay a jagged stone weighing all of a pound. He took it up and held it in readiness.

Closer and closer came Vorlange, turning now to the right and now to the left, for following the trail among the rocks and brush was no easy matter.

"Might as well give yourselves up!" he called out. "I am bound to spot you sooner or later."

To this neither offered any reply, but Dick felt Nellie shiver. They could now see the flare of the torch plainly, for Vorlange was less than thirty feet away.

Presently the spy uttered a low cry of pleasure. He had found several footprints, where Dick had slipped from a rock into the dirt. Now he came straight for them, waving the torch above his head that it might throw its light to a greater distance.

"So there you are!" The man caught sight of Nellie's dress. "I told you I would catch you. It's not such an easy matter to get away from Louis Vorlange. The next time I lock you up--oh!"

A deep groan escaped the spy. Dick had let fly the jagged stone, taking him directly in the forehead and keeling him over like a tenpin. The blow left a deep cut from which the blood flowed in a stream, and Vorlange was completely stunned.

"Oh, Dick, have you--you--killed him?" burst from Nellie's lips, in horror.

"I guess not, Nellie; he's stunned, that's all. Come, let us run for it again--before that Indian changes his mind and comes back."

"You might take his pistol," suggested the quick-witted girl.

"A good idea--I will. Now let me carry you again, I see you can hardly stand on that foot." For Nellie had limped along a dozen steps in great pain.

"But I am so heavy, Dick----"

"Never mind, I can carry you a little distance, at least."

"You had better save yourself and let me go."

"What! Nellie, do you think me so selfish? Never! Come, and we'll escape or die in the attempt."

And catching her up as before, he started off on as rapid a gait as the weight of his fair burden would permit.

A distance of a hundred yards had been covered and Dick found himself ascending a slight hill. The climb was by no means easy, yet he kept on manfully, knowing what capture by Yellow Elk might mean.

"He would tomahawk me and carry Nellie off," he thought, and it would be hard to say which he thought the worst, the tomahawking or the carrying off of the girl for whom he entertained such a high regard.

The top of the hill reached, they saw before them a broad stretch of open prairie, flanked to the north and the south by the woods from which they had just emerged.

"I'll be thrashed if I know where we are," he said. "Have you any idea?"

"No, Dick, I am completely bewildered."

"I wonder if it is safe to attempt to cross this prairie? It is pretty dark, but that redskin has mighty sharp eyes."

"Let us go down to the edge of the woods first and rest a bit. I am sure you are pretty well out of breath, and if I can bathe my ankle in some cold water perhaps I'll be able to walk on it before long."

"Don't try it, Nellie; I'll carry you," and again the youth picked her up.

It was not long before they reached a convenient hollow, where there was a small pool. Here Nellie made herself comfortable and took off the shoe which hurt her so much. Bathed, the ankle which had been twisted felt much better. It was still, however, much swollen, and to walk far on that foot was as yet out of the question.

An hour went by, a quiet hour, in which only the cries of the night birds and the occasional hoot of an owl disturbed them. They conversed in whispers and Dick's ears were ever on the alert, for he felt certain that Vorlange or Yellow Elk would sooner or later continue the search for them.

Nellie was very sleepy and at last her eyes closed and she dropped into a slumber upon Dick's shoulder, forming such a pretty picture the youth could do nothing but admire her. "I'll save her--I must do it!" he murmured, and kissed her wavy tresses softly.

It wanted still two hours to sunrise when he awakened her. She leaped up with a start.

"I have been asleep! Oh, Dick, why did you let me drop off?"

"I knew how tired you must be after going through all you did. But we must be on our way now, before it grows lighter. How is the foot?"

"It is stiff, but much better. Which way shall we go?"

"Let us strike across the prairie and to the north. That is bound to bring us into Kansas sooner or later, and once there we'll be sure to locate the boomers without much trouble."

Both were hungry, but, as there was no food at hand, neither said a word on that point. Getting a drink at a running brook close by, they started off, Dick holding Nellie's hand, that she might not go down on the ankle that was still weak.

Only a corner of the broad prairie passed, and then they turned again into a woods. The sun was now up and it was growing warmer.

"I'll shoot a few birds if I can't find anything else," said Dick. "We can't starve, and birds broiled over a fire will make a fair meal."

"But the noise?" began Nellie.

"I know; but, as I said, we can't starve, Nellie. We'll have to take the risk. Here goes!"

Dick crept forward to where half a dozen birds sat on a nearby bush. The birds were in a flutter over something, but Dick did not notice this. Bringing two of the birds into range for a single shot, he blazed away with his pistol.

The sharp crack of the firearm was still echoing through the woods when there came a roar from behind the bushes the birds had occupied. Dick had brought down his game and more, he had struck a bear in the shoulder. In another moment the huge beast leaped into sight, and with angry eyes and gleaming teeth bore straight for the astonished boy.

CHAPTER XXIII.
THE SOLDIERS AGAIN.

Never was Dick Arbuckle more astonished than when the big bear leaped out from behind the bushes and confronted himself and Nellie Winthrop.

"Oh, Dick! a bear!" screamed the girl, and stood still, too paralyzed with fright to move.

As we know, Dick had just brought down several birds with his pistol--indeed it was this very shot which had clipped the bear--and now the weapon was empty and useless, having had but one chamber loaded.

But as the great beast came forward, Dick knew enough not to stand still. He retreated in double-quick order, and forced Nellie to accompany him. Away they went through the woods with the bear in close pursuit.

At the start of the chase girl and boy were at least forty feet in advance, but despite his bulk the bear made rapid progress, and slowly but surely began to lessen the distance between himself and those he sought to make his victims. Looking over his shoulder, Dick saw him lumbering along, his mouth wide open and his blood-red tongue hanging out as though ready to lick him in.

"I--I--can't run any more," gasped Nellie. Her heart was beating as though ready to break. "Oh, Dick, what shall we do?"

"Here is a tree with low branches--jump for that--I will help you up!" returned the youth, and in a few seconds they were in the tree, a scrub oak, with the big bear underneath, eying them angrily, and speculating upon how he could bring them down within reach of his powerful embrace and his hungry maw.

"He is going to climb up," came from Nellie's lips a few seconds later. She was right. Bruin had attacked the tree trunk and now he was coming up slowly, as though afraid of moving into some trap.

Dick did not answer, for talking would have done no good. He was re-loading the pistol with all possible speed.

Crack! Dick had leaned down through the branches of the oak and taken aim at one of those bloodshot eyes. There was a howl and a roar, and the bear fell down with a crash that shook the forest. As to whether the bullet had found that eye or not Dick could not tell, but certain it was that once on the ground the bear picked himself up in short order and started to run away.

"You hit him!" cried Nellie. "Oh, Dick, if only he don't come back!"

"He's not going away--very far," answered the boy. The shot had encouraged him and his blood was up. A moment later Nellie was horrified to behold him drop to the grass and make off after the beast.

"That bear will kill him sure!" she ejaculated. "Oh, Dick, come back! please do!" she screamed.

A shot answered her, a shot which was quickly followed by another. A minute of painful silence; then suddenly the bear staggered into view with Dick at his heels.

"I've nailed him!" shouted the boy, joyfully, and another shot did the work. With a groan the bear keeled over, gave a jerk or two, and died.

Nellie was in such a tremble she could scarcely descend from the tree. When she did come down she found Dick hard at work cutting out a juicy steak from the bear's flank.

"We'll have a breakfast fit for a king now," he said, with a little laugh, to scatter his former nervousness. "Just wait till I light a fire. I must gather the driest available sticks, so as to make as little smoke as possible."

"Yes, we don't want our enemies to locate us," answered the girl, and saw to it that every twig which went on the blaze which was kindled was as dry as a bone.

In less than half an hour the steak had been done to a turn, and they sat down to eat it. It was certainly a most informal meal, without plates or platter, and only Dick's pocket knife to cut the steak with. Yet neither had ever enjoyed a repast more. Having finished, they procured a drink at a flowing stream behind them, and then Dick cut off a chunk of the bear meat, wrapped it in a bit of skin and slung it over his shoulder.

"We may want another meal of it before we reach civilization," he explained, "Nothing like preparing one's self, when we have the chance."

"It's a shame to leave such a beautiful bear skin robe behind," answered Nellie. "But I suppose it cannot be helped. Oh, if only we were safe once more."

Again they set off on their weary tramp northward, and thus nearly two miles were covered. The sun was now coming out strongly, and Dick saw that his fair companion was beginning to grow tired.

"We will rest a little, Nellie," he said, "I think perhaps we can afford to take it easy now."

"I am so fearful that Indian is following us!" answered the girl with a shudder. "If he should find that bear, and--Oh, Dick, look!"

Nellie leaped to her feet from the seat she had just taken, and pointed behind her. Dick gave one look and his heart sank within him. Yellow Elk was bearing down upon them as swiftly as his long legs would permit!

In his hand the Indian chief carried a gun, and as Nellie arose he caught sight of the pair and pointed the weapon at Dick's head.

"White boy throw down pistol!" he called out, when within speaking distance.

"Let Yellow Elk throw down his gun," answered Dick. His pistol was up and now he shoved Nellie behind him.

"White boy fool--cannot shoot against Yellow Elk," growled the redskin. He had been following their trail since sun-up and was somewhat winded.

"Perhaps I can shoot. Did you see that bear I brought down?" rejoined Dick.

At this the Indian frowned.

"Bear must have been sick--white boy no bring game down like that if well-- too powerful."

"I brought him down and I'll bring you down if you don't stop where you are," was the steady answer.

"Oh, Dick, he'll shoot you," whispered Nellie. She wanted to get before him, but he would not allow it.

By this time Yellow Elk had arrived to within a dozen steps of them. Now he stopped and the frown upon his ugly countenance deepened.

"Did white boy hear what Yellow Elk said?"

"I did."

"Does white boy want to die?"

"Does Yellow Elk want to die? I can shoot as straight as you."

The words had scarcely left Dick's mouth than there came a clear click.

The redskin had fired point-blank at the lad, but the gun had failed to go off, the weapon being an old one the Indian had found at the fort--a gun some soldier had discarded as useless.

Following the click Nellie uttered a scream. Then came a crack as Dick fired, and Yellow Elk uttered a yell of pain, having received a painful wound in the side.

With clubbed gun the Indian now rushed in and a hand-to-hand struggle followed. Dick fought valiantly, but was no match for the tall redskin, and a well-directed blow laid him senseless upon the prairie grass. "You have killed him!" screamed Nellie. She was about to kneel at Dick's side, when Yellow Elk hauled her back.

"White dove come with me--boy no killed--be right by-an-by," said the redskin.

"I will not go with you!" she gasped. "Let me down!" for Yellow Elk had raised her up to his broad shoulder.

The redskin merely smiled grimly and set off on a swift walk, which speedily took both Nellie and himself out of sight of poor Dick.

The girl's heart was almost broken by this swift turn of affairs. She had hoped in a few more hours to be safe among her friends, and here she was once again the captive of the Indian she so much feared.

On and on kept Yellow Elk until the stream was reached upon which was located the log cabin where Nellie had been a prisoner. She wondered if Yellow Elk was going to take her there again, but she asked no questions.

Presently the Indian chief came to a sudden halt and raised his head as if to listen. Nellie listened, too, and at a distance heard the tramp of several men. At once Yellow Elk darted behind a number of bushes.

"White girl make noise Yellow Elk kill!" he hissed into his fair captive's ear, and drew his hunting knife.

The tramp of feet came closer. A detachment of foot soldiers were moving through the woods. Soon they came within sight of the pair.

As they came closer Nellie saw they were Government troops. A prisoner was between them--a man. It was Jack Rasco.

"Uncle Jack!" she moaned, when Yellow Elk clapped his hand over her mouth and pointed the hunting knife at her throat.

"Hush!" he commanded, but this was unnecessary, for the discovery and her great fear had caused Nellie to swoon. She fell back, and for a long while she knew no more.

In the meantime Dick had slowly recovered consciousness. The blow had been a fearful one, and long after he sat up he was unable to rise to his feet, so shaky was he in the legs. Slowly the realization of what had occurred came back to him.

"Gone--poor Nellie!" he gasped, and braced himself as best he could. Gazing around he saw that neither girl nor redskin was in sight. Without delay he started to search for Yellow Elk's trail.

He was loping along over the prairies when a shout from his left struck upon his ears. As he gazed in the direction he beheld a number of soldiers swooping down upon him. These were the men who had Jack Rasco a prisoner, the cavalrymen having turned the man of the plains over to them. In a moment Dick was surrounded.

"Jack!" cried the youth, and rushed up to Rasco. "What does this mean?"

"It means I'm a prisoner," answered Rasco, sadly. "Have you seen anything of Nellie?"

In a moment Dick had told his story, to which the soldiers as well as Rasco listened closely. At once several of the guard were sent off to hunt up the redskin, if it were possible to do so. Rasco wanted to go along, but his request was refused.

"You'll slip us if you get the chance," said the officer in charge. "You'll go to the fort. And I fancy the boy will go, too, since he seems to belong to the boomers."

And against his earnest protestations Dick was made to accompany the soldiers, being bound hand to hand with the man of the plains.

An hour later the soldiers' camp was reached, and Rasco and Dick were placed in a temporary guard house. They had been there but a short while when a visitor entered. It was--Louis Vorlange!

"So they have you safe, I see," began Vorlange, when Rasco sprang at him and knocked him down.

"Will you make my niece a prisoner," he cried, wrathfully, for Dick had told him the story. "You dirty spy!"

"Hold up," gasped Vorlange, his face growing white. "Rasco, don't be a fool. I--I--made her a prisoner because I have orders to arrest anybody found roaming around----"

"I won't argy the p'int!" roared Rasco. "I know you, Vorlange, and so does Dick here. You robbed and nearly murdered thet boy's father!"

At these words Vorlange staggered back as though struck a blow.

"Who says I--I did that?" he faltered.

"I say so."

"And so do I," put in Dick, boldly. "We'll have a nice story to tell when we are brought out for examination, I'll tell you that."

Vorlange breathed hard and glared from one to the other. Then of a sudden he caught Dick by the arm and turned him to one side.

"Boy, beware how you cross me," he hissed into Dick's ears. "Beware, I say! I have known your father for years, and I have the knowledge in my possession which can send your father to the gallows."

CHAPTER XXIV.
CHASED BY CAVALRY.

Checkmated! By Jove, but this is too bad."

Such were the words which issued from Pawnee Brown's lip as he swung around and saw the cavalrymen sitting on their horses at attention.

His disappointment was keen. In speaking of it afterwards he said:

"I never felt so bad in my life. I had promised to take the boomers through and I felt that I had disappointed nearly four thousand people who were looking to me with utmost confidence."

But disappointment was not the worst of it. Hardly had the command to halt been issued than the captain of the troops advanced toward the scout.

"Pawnee Brown!" he ejaculated, in surprise, and a smile of satisfaction crossed his face. "This is a great pleasure."

"Is it?" answered the great scout, coldly.

"It is indeed. Do you intend to throw up your hands?"

For the scout's hands had not yet been lifted skyward.

"This looks as if you meant to arrest me, captain."

"Why shouldn't I? You are at the head of the Kansas boomers, are you not?"

"I have that honor, yes."

"It's a question to me if it is an honor. You are transgressing the laws of the United States when you try to get into Oklahoma for homestead purposes."

"Say rather that we transgress the laws of the cattle kings, captain. Under the U. S. Homestead Law we have a perfect right to this land, if we can get in and stake our claims, and you know it."

"I know nothing of the sort. This talk about the cattle kings is all nonsense!" roared the cavalry officer. He knew Pawnee Brown was more than half right, but felt he must obey the orders he had received from his superiors. "I'll have to take you to the fort."

"All right, take me--if you can, captain," came the quick answer. "Don't you dare fire on me, for you know I am a crack shot and I promise I'll fire on you in return and lay you low!"

Thus speaking, the boomer wheeled about and sent Bonnie Bird off like a shot along the trail he had come.

The movement was so quick that for the moment the cavalry officer was paralyzed and knew not what to do. He raised his long pistol, but Pawnee Brown's stern threat rang in his ears and he hesitated about using the weapon, having no desire to be laid low.

"After him, men!" he roared, upon recovering his wits. "We must capture him!"

"Shall we fire, cap'n?" came from several, and a number of shining pistol barrels were leveled toward the great scout.

"N--no, capture him alive," came the hesitating reply; and away went the calvary men at a breakneck speed in pursuit.

Looking back over his shoulder, Pawnee saw them coming. To lessen the chances of being shot, he bent low over his faithful mare's neck.

"On, Bonnie, on!" he cried softly, and the beautiful animal seemed to understand that it was a race for life and death.

"Crack!" It was the report of a pistol close at hand. Looking among the trees, Pawnee Brown saw an arm wearing the colors of a cavalryman disappearing among the foliage of a nearby tree. He aimed his own weapon and pulled the trigger. A yell of pain followed.

The marksman had been Tucker, the fellow hired to take the great scout's life. Tucker had been on picket duty for the cavalry troop, but had failed to note Pawnee Brown's first movement in that direction. Seeing the scout coming, he had instantly thought of the promised reward and taken aim. The bullet had struck Pawnee Brown's shoulder, merely, however, scraping the skin. On the return fire Tucker was hit in the side and nearly broke his neck in a tumble backward into a hole behind him.

The chase was not of long duration. Although they had good steeds, not one of the cavalryman's horses could gain upon the scout's sturdy racing mare, and soon they dropped further and further behind. Seeing this, Pawnee Brown turned to the eastward, out of the ravine, and in three minutes had his pursuers entirely off the trail.

His face grew thoughtful as he allowed Bonnie Bird to drop into a walk. The cavalry had followed the wagon train westward--they were bound to keep the boomers in sight. What was to be done? Should he advise another movement during the night to come and then a forward dash?

"We might make it," he mused. "But if we did not there would be a fearful fight and possibly slaughter. I wish I knew just how matters were going at Washington."

Pawnee Brown had friends at the Capital, men who were doing their best to defeat the cattle kings by having a bill passed in Congress opening Oklahoma to settlement--a bill that would smooth the present difficulty for all concerned. He felt that the bill was not needed, yet it would be better to have such a law than to have some of the boomers killed before their rights could be established.

"I'll send a messenger off to the nearest telegraph station and telegraph for the news," he went on. "A day's delay may mean many lives saved. It shall never be said that Pawnee Brown rushed in, heedless of the danger to those who trusted in him."

It was not long before the scout reached the boomers' camp. Here he found several waiting for him.

"I want to see Pawnee Brown." It was Dan Gilbert, who was making his way through the crowd to the great scout's side. Gilbert held a message from Arkansas City. It was to the effect that Pawnee Brown should telegraph to Washington at once and wait until noon at Arkansas City for a reply.

Five minutes later Pawnee Brown was on the trail over which the wagon train had journeyed the night before. He had told Gilbert, Clemmer and the others of the nearness of the Government cavalrymen and had advised a halt until further orders from himself. Clemmer had promised to wait, although ready "ter swoop down on 'em, b' gosh, an' take wot belongs ter us," as he expressed himself.

The ride back to Arkansas City was an uneventful one, and arriving there, Pawnee Brown lost no time in visiting the telegraph office.

"A message for you," said the operator, and handed it over.

It was from Washington and stated: "The Oklahoma bill is now before the Lower House; wait for more news."

"I'm glad we've woke up those politicians at Washington," murmured the scout, and then wrote out a telegram in reply.

There was now nothing to do but to wait, and impatient as he was to rejoin the boomers, Pawnee Brown had to content himself until another message should reach him. To make the time pass more quickly the great scout went around to a number of places buying supplies that were much needed.

An hour later he found himself on the outskirts of the city, whence he had come to look up several wagons, to replace some that had broken down. He was galloping along on horseback when the sight of two men quarreling near the open doorway of a deserted barn caught his eye, and impelled by something which was more than curiosity, he turned in from the road to see how the quarrel might end. As he came closer he saw that one of the men was Mortimer Arbuckle!

"Hullo, what can this mean?" he cried, softly. "I thought Dick's father was still in bed from the effects of that dastardly night's work. Who can that stranger be?"

Dismounting, he tied Bonnie Bird to a tree and came forward, but in line with the barn, that he might not be seen. Soon he was within easy hearing distance of all that was being said.

"I want to know what brought you out here, Dike Powell?" he heard Mr. Arbuckle say in excited tones. "Did you follow me?"

"No, I did not, Arbuckle," came in reply. "What makes you think I did?"

"I was knocked down and robbed but a few nights ago, and my most valuable papers, as well as my money, were taken from me."

"Do you mean to insinuate that I am a thief?" cried Dike Powell.

"You are none too good for it. I have not forgotten how you used to sneak around my office in New York after information concerning my Western mining claims."

"You're getting mighty sharp, Arbuckle."

"I hope I am. I used to feel queer in my head at times, but--but--I think I am growing better of that."

As he spoke Mortimer Arbuckle drew his white hand across his forehead.

The attack and the adventure on the river had been fearful, but it really looked as if they were going to prove of benefit to him. His eyes were brighter than they had been for many a day. Pawnee Brown noticed, too, that his manner of talking was more direct than he usually employed.

"I hope for the boy's sake his mind is clearing," he thought.

"I think you are growing more queer--to accuse me," said Dike Powell. "I never harmed you."

"I know better. While I was on my back I thought it all over. Dike Powell, you are a villain, and if ever I get the chance I'll turn you over to the police. You have followed me to the West, and for no good purpose. I will unmask you."

"Will you? Not much!"

Thus speaking, Dike Powell leaped forward. He was a powerful man, and catching Mortimer Arbuckle by the throat, he would have borne the semi-invalid to the floor had not Pawnee Brown interfered.

There was a rush and a crack, as the scout's fist met Dike Powell's ear, and over the man rolled, to bring up against the side of the barn with a crash.

"Who--who hit me?" spluttered the rascal, as, half dazed, he staggered to his feet. "If I--Pawnee Brown!"

"Dike Powell!" ejaculated the scout, as he saw the fellow full in the face for the first time. "Where have you been these long years?"

"Oh, Pawnee, how glad I am that you came in," panted Mortimer Arbuckle, sinking down upon an old feed box. "The villain was--was----"

"I saw it all, Arbuckle; rest yourself. I will take care of this forger."

"Forger!" came simultaneously from Mortimer Arbuckle and from his assailant, but in different tones of voice. "Do you then know Dike Powell?"

"Yes, I know him as Powell Dike, a forger, who fled from Peoria a dozen years ago. And what do you know of him?"

"I know him as a Wall street sneak--a man who was forever hanging around, trying to get information out of which he might make a few dollars. I have accused him of following me to the West. I am inclined to think he robbed me----"

"I did not," ejaculated Powell Dike, for such really was his name.

"I believe you," replied Pawnee Brown. He had spoken to Dick and Rasco of this man. "But you know who did rob Mortimer Arbuckle," he went on, significantly.

"I--I--do not," answered Powell Dike, but his lips trembled.

"You lie, Dike. Now tell the truth."

Pawnee Brown saw the manner of man he had to deal with and tapped his pistol. Instantly Powell Dike fell upon his knees.

"Don't--don't shoot me!" he whined. "I'll tell all--everything. I am not dead positive, but--but I guess Louis Vorlange robbed Arbuckle."

Pawnee Brown looked at Mortimer Arbuckle to see what effect this declaration might have upon Dick's father. He saw the ex-stock broker start forward in amazement. Then he faltered, threw up his hands, and fell forward in a dead faint!

CHAPTER XXV.
GOOD NEWS FROM WASHINGTON.

Fainted, by Jove!"

So spoke Pawnee Brown as he sprang forward to Mortimer Arbuckle's aid. The man was as pale as the driven snow, and for the instant the great scout thought his very heart had stopped beating.

He raised Mortimer Arbuckle up and opened his collar and took off his tie, that he might get some air.

"Wot's the row here?"

It was the voice of Peter Day, the backwoodsman who had agreed to take care of Arbuckle during his illness. He had followed the man out of the house to see that no harm might befall him.

"He has fainted," answered Pawnee Brown. "Fetch some water, and hold that--hang it, he's gone!"

Pawnee Brown rushed to the barn door. Far away he saw Powell Dike running as though the old Nick was after him. A second later the rascal disappeared from view. The boomer never saw or heard of him again.

Between the great scout and Pawnee Brown, Mortimer Arbuckle was once again taken to Day's home and made comfortable.

"He insisted on taking a walk to-day," explained the backwoodsman. "I told him he couldn't stand it. I reckon he's as bad now as he ever was."

"Take good care of him, Day, and beware of any men who may be prowling about," answered Pawnee Brown. "There is something wrong in the air, but I'm satisfied that if we help this poor fellow we'll be on the right side of the brush."

Mortimer Arbuckle was now coming around, but when he spoke he was quite out of his mind. The doctor was hastily sent for, and he administered a potion which speedily put the sufferer to sleep.

"It's an odd case," said the medical man. "The fellow is suffering more mentally than physically. He must have something awful on his mind."

"He is the victim of some plot--I am certain of it," was the scout's firm answer.

Not long after this, Pawnee Brown was returning to Arkansas City, certain that Mortimer Arbuckle would now be well cared for and closely watched until he and Dick could return to the sufferer.

"As soon as this booming business is over I must try to clear things for that old gent," murmured the boomer to himself as he rode up to the telegraph office. "I'd do a good deal for him and that noble son of his."

Another telegram had just come in, by way of Wichita, which ran as follows:

"The Lower House of Congress has passed the Oklahoma bill. Pawnee Brown has woke the politicians up at last. Stand ready to enter Oklahoma if an attempt is made to throw the bill aside in the Senate, but don't be rash, as it may not be long before everything comes our way--in fact, it looks as if everything would come very soon."

At this telegram the great scout was inclined to throw up his hat and give a cheer. His work in Kansas was having an effect. No longer could the cattle kings stand up against the rights of the people. He handed the message to a number of his friends standing near.

"Hurrah fer Pawnee Brown!" shouted one man, and standing on a soap box read the telegram aloud.

"Score one fer the boomers!"

"An' a big one fer Pawnee."

"Don't hurry now, Pawnee, you've got 'em whar the hair ez good an' long!"

"It would seem so, men," answered the great scout. "No, I'll be careful now--since the tide has turned. In less than sixty days I'll wager all I am worth we'll march into Oklahoma without the first sign of trouble."

It did not take the news long to travel to the boomers' camp, and great was the rejoicing upon every side.

"Dot's der pest ding I vos hear for a month," said Humpendinck. "Pawnee ought to haf a medal alreatty."

"It's a stattoo we will put up fer him in Oklahomy," said Delaney. "A stattoo wid Pawnee a-ridin' loike mad to the new lands, wid the Homestead act in wan hand an' a bundle o' sthakes in th' other, an' under the stattoo we'll put the wur-ruds, 'Pawnee Brown, the St. Patrick av Oklahomy!'"

"Ach! go on mit yer St. Patrick!" howled Humpendinck. "He vos noddings but a snake killer."

"Oh, mon!" burst in Rosy Delaney. "A snake killer, Moike, do ye moind thot? Swat the Dootchman wan, quick!"

And Mike "swatted" with an end of a fence rail he was chopping up for fire-wood. But Humpendinck dodged, and Rosy caught the blow, and there followed a lively row between her and Mike, in the midst of which the German boomer sneaked away.

"Dot Irishmans vos so fiery as der hair mit his head," he muttered to himself. "I dink I vos keep out of sight bis he vos cool off, and den--Mine gracious, Bumpkin, var did you come from? I dinks you vos left behind py Arkansas City."

For there had suddenly appeared before Humpendinck the form of the dunce, hatless and with his black hair tumbled over his face in all directions.

"Ha, ha! where have I been?" cried Pumpkin. "Where haven't I been you had better ask. I've been everywhere--among the soldiers and the boomers and the In-dians." He stopped short. "Where is Pawnee Brown?"

"Ofer py Clemmer's vagon. But he ton't vont ter pother mit you now."

"He will bother with me," and so speaking Pumpkin ran off, to reach the great scout's side and pluck him by the coat sleeve.

"At your service, sir," he said, bowing low, for with all of his peculiarities Pumpkin had a great respect for Pawnee Brown.

"What is it, lad?"

"I have to report, sir, that your pard is captured--Jack Rasco; he had a fearful fight and the soldiers have him. Ha! ha! they will shoot Jack--if you let 'em, but I know you won't--will you now?"

"You are certain Jack is captured?"

"Dead sure--saw him with my own eyes. Ha! ha! they tried to catch Pumpkin, but they might as well try to catch a ghost. Ha! ha! but I give 'em a fine run."

It took a good deal of talking to get a straight story from the half-witted youth, but at last Pawnee Brown was in full possession of the facts. Pumpkin had seen Rasco on the march just before Dick was taken.

Immediately after this the boomer held a short consultation with Clemmer.

"I feel it my duty to help Rasco to escape, if it can be done," he said. "Besides, it is high time for me to return to Dick Arbuckle and to find out, if possible, what has become of Jack's niece."

"Shall I go along?" questioned Clemmer, "I wouldn't like anything better."

"All right, come on," answered the great scout.

He had scarcely spoken when a loud cry rang out, coming from the lower end of the camp.

"Buckley's bull has broken loose! Look out for yourself, the beast has gone mad!"

"Buckley's bull!" muttered Pawnee Brown. "I ordered him to slaughter that vicious beast. Why, he's as fierce as those the Mexicans use in their bull fights!"

"He's a terror," answered Clemmer. "If he--By gum, here he comes, Pawnee!"

As he spoke Clemmer turned to one side and started to run. Looking forward the great scout saw the bull bearing down upon him. The eyes of the creature were bloodshot and the foam was dripping from the corners of his mouth, showing that he was clearly beyond control.

The bull, which was of extra large size, had Clemmer in view, and made after the cowboy, who happened to be unarmed. Away went man and beast in something of a circle, to fetch up near Pawnee Brown less than a minute later. As they came close, Clemmer fell and went sprawling almost at the scout's feet.

"Save me!" he panted. "Save me, Pawnee!"

Pawnee Brown did not answer. Leaping over the cowboy's prostrate form, he pulled out his pistol and his hunting knife and stood ready to receive the bull, who came tearing along, with lowered horns, ready to charge the scout to the death.

CHAPTER XXVI.
THE BOOMER AND THE BULL.

For the moment it looked as if Pawnee Brown meant to let the mad bull gore him to pieces.

On and on came the beast until less than two yards separated him and the great scout.

Crack! came the report of the boomer's pistol, and the bull fell back a pace, clipped between the horns. A lucky swerve downward had saved him from a bullet wound through the eye.

There was no time for another shot. With a bellow the bull leaped the intervening space and landed almost on top of Pawnee Brown!

A yell went up from those who saw the movement.

"Pawnee is done fur. The bull will rip him inside out."

"Buckley ought to have killed that bull long ago--that's the second time he's gone on a rampage."

"Somebody shoot him and save Pawnee!"

The last was a well meant cry, but a shot could not be thought of, for man and beast were too close together.

But Pawnee Brown was not yet defeated. He still held his trusty hunting knife, and he was not terrorized as some of the onlookers imagined.

A few words will explain the cause. In his day the scout had visited Mexico more than once, and while there had participated in more than one bull fight, on one occasion defeating a celebrated Mexican fighter and gaining a handsome prize.

As the mad bull charged, the scout leaped like lightning to one side, and drove the hunting knife up to the hilt into the beast's throat.

There was a spurt of blood, a bellow of pain, and the bull staggered back several steps.

He was badly wounded, but by no means out of the fight, as his glaring eyes still showed. He shook his head vigorously, then charged again.

Once more the knife went up and came down, this time just below the beast's ear. A fearful bellow came after the stroke. Before the bull could retire, the knife was withdrawn and plunged in a third and last time. This third stroke wound up the encounter, for limping to one side the bull fell forward upon his knees, gave a kick or two with his hind legs, and rolled over on the prairie grass, dead.

"Hurrah! Pawnee has killed him."

"Talk about yer bull fighters! They ain't in it with Pawnee!"

"Yer saved my life," exclaimed Clemmer, who had risen. "I shan't forget yer, Pawnee," and he held out his broad hand for a shake.

The bull dead, Pawnee Brown called Buckley up and gave him a lecture for not having killed the vicious beast long ago.

"You have no business to bring such a bull into camp in the first place, Buckley," he said. "Be more careful in the future, or you'll have to get out, bag and baggage. That bull might have killed half a dozen people had he charged the crowd."

A short while after this the great scout and Clemmer set off from Honnewell along the ravine in search of Dick, Rasco and Nellie Winthrop. The cheering news from Washington had set Pawnee Brown at rest so far as his duty to the boomers was concerned, and he felt quite free to pursue his own affairs and those of his immediate friends.

"If possible I would like to meet Louis Vorlange and have a talk with him," he said to Clemmer, after having related what had occurred near Peter Day's home. "I think that spy can clear up much of this mystery concerning Mortimer Arbuckle, if he will."

"It ain't likely he'll open his trap," answered Clemmer. "By doin' thet he'd only be gettin' himself in hot water."

"We'll make him speak," was Pawnee Brown's grim response.

An hour of hard riding brought them to the spot where Dick had been left. Not a single trace of the lad could be found. Both men looked blank.

"Bet he's wandered off and got lost," said Clemmer, and Pawnee Brown nodded.

"We'll strike off eastward, Cal, and see if we can't find some trace of him. It is no use of going westward. If he had gone that way, he would have reached the ravine and come up into Kansas."

Once again they set off. An hour was spent here and there, when suddenly Clemmer uttered a cry.

"Been a struggle hyer, Pawnee. See them footprints?"

"Three people," answered the scout, making an inspection. "A boy, a girl or a woman, and an Indian. Can they have been Dick, Nellie Winthrop and Yellow Elk? Hang me if it doesn't look like it."

"Hyer's where the trail leads off," said Clemmer. "And that's the boy's. Can't see nuthin' o' the gal's."

"That means the Indian carried her off," ejaculated Pawnee Brown. "Let us follow his trail without delay."

"But the boy's?"

"You follow that, and I'll follow the redskin. If he had the girl I want to know it."

A few words more and they separated. Pawnee Brown was on his mettle and followed Yellow Elk's trail with all the keenness of an Indian himself. In half an hour he had reached the brook. Here he came to a series of rocks and was forced to come to a halt.

But not for long. Fording the water-course, he began a search which speedily revealed the trail again, leading to a small river a quarter of a mile further on.

He followed the river for less than fifty feet, when a number of voices broke upon his ears.

"I'm sure I saw the redskin on the river, and he had a girl with him, Ross."

"You must have been dreaming, Tucker. No redskins up here."

"All right, I know what I am talking about."

"I think I saw something, too," said a third voice, that of Skimmy, the calvary man.

The three calvary men were out on a scouting expedition, to learn if the boomers were in the vicinity of the river.

Tucker especially was on the lookout for Pawnee Brown, determined to bring the great scout down and thus win the reward Louis Vorlange had promised.

The scout listened to the talk of the cavalrymen for fully ten minutes with great interest.

He had just started to move on, satisfied that it would be of no benefit to remain longer, when Tucker turned and walked his horse directly toward the spot where he was concealed.

"A boomer behind the brush!" shouted the cavalryman. "Come, boys, and take him!"

Immediately there was a rush, and Pawnee Brown was surrounded. He had his pistol out and in return came the weapons of the trio.

"Well, gentlemen, you seem to want to make me your prisoner," said the scout, coolly.

"Thet's wot," cried Ross. "Eh, Tucker?"

To make Pawnee Brown a prisoner would be of no personal benefit to him.

"You seem to bear me a grudge," said the boomer, eying him sharply.

Tucker could not stand that gaze and his eyes dropped.

"Yes, you're a prisoner," said Ross. "Let's bind him up, Skimmy."

"Take that!"

Pawnee Brown leaped forward and hurled both Ross and Skimmy to the ground. Ere they could rise he had turned upon Tucker. The tall calvary man had his pistol cocked, and now he blazed away almost in Pawnee Brown's face, and then both went down, with the scout on top.

The flash of the pistol had scorched the boomer's skin, but the bullet sung over his head, missing him by less than an inch. As he came down upon Tucker he hit the cavalryman a terrific blow in the jaw, breaking that member and knocking out several teeth.

"On him!" yelled Skimmy, and tried to rise. But now Pawnee Brown was again up, and flung Skimmy on top of Ross. In a moment more he was running along the river bank.

He was almost out of sight, when there came two shots, from Ross and Skimmy. Neither hit him, however, and he continued on his way, while the two cavalrymen turned back to pick up Tucker, who lay in a heap, groaning and twisting from intense pain. The tall cavalryman could not, of course, talk, and his wound was so serious that there was nothing to do but to carry him to his horse, support him in the saddle and ride back to the fort for medical assistance. It was a clean knock-out, and one that Tucker had good cause to remember to the day of his death.

It was some time ere Pawnee Brown struck the trail of Yellow Elk again, but having once spotted it he pursued his course with increased vigor. The trail led along the river to where there was almost a lake. This had just been reached, when he heard a scream. Instantly he recognized Nellie Winthrop's voice.

"Thank heaven I came as soon as I did," he murmured, and dashed forward to the spot from whence the sound had proceeded.

CHAPTER XXVII.
THE LAST OF YELLOW ELK.

When Nellie Winthrop recovered sufficiently to realize what was going on around her, she found herself upon Yellow Elk's back, with her hands tied together at the wrists behind her.

Away went the redskin until the vicinity where the encounter with Dick had occurred was left far behind.

The brook crossed, the Indian chief set off for the river. Not once did he stop or speak until a pond was gained.

Beyond the pond was a shelter of trees, growing in a circle which was about fifteen feet in diameter. Against the trees the brush had been piled, forming a rude hut.

Taking Nellie inside of this shelter, Yellow Elk deposited her on the ground. Of the cord which bound her hands there were several feet left, and this end he wound around a tree and tied fast.

"Now white girl no run away," he grinned. "Stay here now until Yellow Elk ready to let her go."

To this she made no answer, for what would be the use of talking to such a fierce creature? She looked at his hideously painted face and shivered.

Yellow Elk now went off, to be gone a long while. When he came back he found her so tired she could scarcely stand beside the tree. She had tried to free herself from her bonds but failed, and a tiny stream of blood was running from one of her tender wrists.

"Yellow Elk got horse now," said the redskin. "We ride now--go many miles."

"Where to?" she faltered.

"Never mind where--white girl come on."

Yellow Elk's manner was so fierce she was frightened more than ever. The Indian had stolen a horse and he had also stolen a lot of "fire-water," and this drink was beginning to make him ugly. He drew out his hunting knife.

"White girl got to become Yellow Elk's squaw!" he cried, brandishing the knife before her face. "No marry Yellow Elk me cut out her heart wid dis!"

At this Nellie gave a shriek and it was this which was borne to the ears of Pawnee Brown.

"Crying do white girl no good," growled the redskin. "Come with me."

"I will not go another foot," and Nellie began to struggle. The Indian chief upbraided her roundly in his own language and ended by raising his knife over her once more.

"Help!" cried Nellie, and a moment later Pawnee Brown burst into view. A glance showed him the true situation, and without hesitation he fired at Yellow Elk.

His bullet clipped across the redskin's chest. By this time Yellow Elk had his own pistol out, and standing erect he aimed straight for the boomer's heart.

Nellie screamed, and knowing nothing else to do, gave the Indian a vigorous shove in the side, which destroyed the aim and made the bullet fly wide of the mark.

In a second more the two men were at it in a hand-to-hand encounter each trying his best to get at the other with his hunting knife, being too close together to use a pistol. As Pawnee Brown afterward said:

"It was Yellow Elk's life or mine, and I made up my mind that it should not be mine--I considered myself worth a good deal more than that worthless redskin."

A cut and a slash upon each side, and the two broke. Yellow Elk had had enough of the fight, and now ran for it in sudden fear. He did not take to the river shore, but skirted the pond and began to ascend a slight hill, beyond which was another fork of the ravine which has figured so largely in our story.

"Let him go! he may kill you!" called out Nellie, when she saw Pawnee Brown start in pursuit. But the scout paid no attention to her. His blood was up and he was determined to either exterminate Yellow Elk or bring him to terms.

The top of the hill was reached. Yellow Elk paused, not knowing exactly how to proceed. Looking back, he saw Pawnee Brown preparing to fire upon him. A pause, and he attempted to leap down to a ledge below him. His foot caught in the roots of a bush and over he went into a deep hollow headlong. There was a sickening thud, a grunt, and all became quiet.

Yellow Elk had paid the death penalty at last.

When Pawnee Brown managed to climb down to the Indian's side, to make certain the wily redskin was not shamming, he found Yellow Elk stone dead, his neck having been completely broken by his fall. He lay on his back, his right hand still clutching his bloody hunting knife.

"Gone now," murmured the great scout. His face softened for an instant. "Hang it all, why must even a redskin be so all-fired bad? If he had wanted to, Yellow Elk might have made a man of himself. I can't stop to bury him, and yet----Hullo, what are those papers sticking out of his pocket?"

The boomer had caught sight of a large packet which had been concealed in Yellow Elk's bosom. He took up the packet and looked it over. It consisted of half a dozen legal-looking documents and twice that number of letters, some addressed to Mortimer Arbuckle and some addressed to Louis Vorlange.

He read over the letters and documents with interest. Those of Dick's father related to the mine in Colorado and were evidently those stolen by Louis Vorlange upon the night of the opening of this tale. The letters belonging to the government spy were epistles addressed to Vorlange from a former friend and partner in various shady transactions. Of these we will hear more later.

"Yellow Elk must have robbed Vorlange of these," mused the great scout, as he rammed the packet in his pocket. In this he was right. Vorlange had dropped the packet by accident and the Indian had failed to restore it, there having been, as the reader knows, no love lost between the two rascals.

Having placed the dead body among the bushes in a little hollow, Pawnee Brown climbed out of the ravine again and rejoined Nellie, who was growing impatient regarding his welfare. The story of what had happened to Yellow Elk was soon told, the scout softening out the ghastly details. Then, to change the subject, he asked her if she knew her uncle was a prisoner of the soldiers.

"Yes," she replied. "Oh, sir, what will they do with him?"

"I don't believe they can do much, Nellie," he answered. "According to the news from Washington, everything is to be smoothed out, and of course the government will have no case against any of us."

"Can I get to my uncle from here? Where is he?"

"About five miles from here. Yes, we can get to him if we want to." Pawnee Brown mused for a moment. "I'll risk it," he said, half aloud. "They can't arrest me for coming to expose a criminal, and I have the facts right here in my pocket."

A moment later he was riding the horse Yellow Elk had stolen, while Nellie was seated upon Bonnie Bird. In this manner they struck out for the agency, called by the soldiers a fort.

About three miles had been covered, when suddenly there came a shout from a thicket to one side of them.

"The cavalry!" gasped Nellie. "What shall we do?"

"Take it coolly, Nellie. I have a winning card this trip," smiled the great scout.

A few seconds later half a dozen fine looking men rode forward, a well-known official of the Indian Territory at their head.

"Pawnee Brown!" ejaculated the official, on recognizing the scout. "It would seem we had made quite a capture. What are you doing with Sergeant Morris' horse?"

"Is this the animal?"

"It is.

"I found him in the possession of a runaway Indian, Yellow Elk. If he is your property you are welcome to him," and Pawnee Brown leaped to the ground.

"Humph! That is all right, but what are you doing here? Don't you know you are on forbidden ground?"

The scout's coolness was a great surprise to the official.

"I would be--under ordinary circumstances, sir. But just now I am on a mission to the agency: a mission I am convinced you will not attempt to hinder."

"What is it?"

"I wish to expose a great criminal, a man who is now in the active service of the United States, although he ought to be in prison or on the gallows."

The official was much surprised.

"I would like to know some of the particulars, Pawnee."

"Are you bound for the agency?"

"Yes."

"Then we will go together, and you can see what takes place. It will probably be well worth your while."

"This is no trick--I know you are itching to get into Oklahoma."

"I will give you my word of honor, sir. I have received word from Washington, and I feel certain that ere long this whole matter will be settled to our mutual satisfaction. In the meantime, booming can wait," and Pawnee Brown smiled in a quiet way.

A few words more followed, and Nellie was introduced. Then the whole party set off on a gallop for the agency, where was to be enacted the last scene in this little drama of the southwest.

CHAPTER XXVIII.
CLEARING UP A MYSTERY--CONCLUSION.

As Vorlange uttered his dire threat into Dick's ear, the boy turned pale and staggered against the wall of his prison.

"Wot's that yer sayin'?" demanded Jack Rasco, who plainly saw the changed look upon his companion's features.

"It is none of your business, Rasco," muttered the spy. "I told the boy; that's enough."

Dick breathed hard. Part of that mystery of the past was out at last. His father was accused of murder--Vorlange held the evidence against him. Like a flash came back to him several things he had almost forgotten. He remembered how on more than one occasion his father had sent money to the West after a letter had come which had upset him greatly. That must have been hush money, to keep this rascal quiet.

"I--I--do not believe you!" he cried in a faint tone. "My father is as upright as any gentleman in the land."

"Is he?" sneered Vorlange. "All right, if you think so, just drive me to the wall and see."

"Where was this crime committed?"

"In Creede, Colorado--at the time the camp was started."

"Who was killed?"

"A miner named Rickwell. He was once a partner of a man named Burch, of whom you have no doubt heard ere this."

"Yes, Burch left us the property you know all about, since you stole the deeds to it. Louis Vorlange, you are playing a deep part but you cannot make me swallow your statements about my father."

"Do you want me to expose him?"

"We'll see about that later. Rasco and I will certainly try to show you up for what you really are."

"Very well," blustered Vorlange. "Your father is a murderer, and he shall swing for it--unless you keep your mouth shut. I----"

Footsteps outside of the prison interrupted Louis Vorlange. An instant later Pawnee Brown and half a dozen others stepped inside of the apartment.

"Pawnee Brown!" cried Dick and Rasco together.

"Are you a prisoner, too?" continued the boy.

"Hardly," smiled the great scout. Then he noticed Vorlange. "Just the men we are after."

"Me?" ejaculated the spy.

"Yes, you."

"What do you want of me, Pawnee Brown? I want nothing to do with such as you--a thieving, low-down boomer--who--oh!"

Vorlange ended with a yell, for Pawnee Brown had caught him by the ear and almost jerked him off his feet.

"Let up! Let up! Oh!"

"Now keep quiet Vorlange," said the scout sternly. "You can thank your stars that I didn't put a bullet through you for letting your tongue run so loosely."

"Thet's so, b'gosh," was Rasco's comment. "But say, Pawnee, he's a reg'lar snake in the grass."

"I know it." Pawnee Brown looked at Dick. "Has he been threatening you, lad?"

"Yes; threatened me and my father, too."

"Have no fear of him, Dick. Louis Vorlange, you have about reached the end of your rope."

"What do you mean?" and the spy's lips quivered as he spoke.

"I mean that I am here to expose you." Pawnee Brown turned to the others who had come in. "Gentlemen, let me introduce to you Louis Vorlange, alias Captain Mull, once of Creede, Colorado."

"Captain Mull!" exclaimed several. "Do you mean the Captain Mull that was wanted for several shady doings, Pawnee?"

"The same Captain Mull, gentlemen."

"It is a--a lie!" screamed Louis Vorlange, but his looks belied him.

"It is the truth, gentlemen, he is the man who once sported under the name of Captain Mull. But that is not all."

"What else, Pawnee?"

"Some years ago a man by the name of Andrew Rickwell was murdered in the Last Chance hotel at Creede. At that time Creede was but a small place and Captain Mull ran the hotel. Who murdered Rickwell was not discovered. But he had occupied a room with another man, a mining agent from New York named Mortimer Arbuckle, the father of this lad here, and some thought Arbuckle had done the foul deed, and he had to run away to escape the fury of a mob. The horror of this occurrence unbalanced the man's mind and to this day he sometimes thinks he may be guilty. But he is innocent."

"He is guilty!" shrieked Louis Vorlange. "I saw him do the deed!"

"I see you acknowledge you were in Creede at that time," answered Pawnee Bill, and Vorlange staggered back over the bad break he had made. "As I said, Mortimer Arbuckle is innocent. There is the murderer, and here are the documents to prove it--and to prove more--that Vorlange is a thief, that he assaulted Mortimer Arbuckle in the dark and left him for dead, and that he is now acting against the best interests of the United States government."

As Pawnee Brown ended he pointed at Vorlange, and held aloft the packet he had taken from Yellow Elk.

"My father's documents!" cried Dick.

"The letters!" shrieked Louis Vorlange. Then he made a sudden leap to secure them, but Pawnee Brown was too quick for him. The scout turned to the captain of cavalry standing near.

"You had better arrest him before he tries to escape."

"They shall not arrest me!" came from Louis Vorlange's set lips. "Clear the way!"

Like a flash his pistol came up and he fired into the crowd, which parted in surprise and let him pass. But not more than ten steps were covered when Pawnee Brown caught him by the arm and threw him headlong to the ground. At the same time the prison sentry fired, and Vorlange was mortally wounded in the side.

"I'll not forget you!" he cried to Pawnee Brown. "But for you I would have lived in clover the balance of my life!" Then he fell into a faint from which he recovered presently, to linger for several days in terrible anguish, dying at last in convulsions.

With the death of Vorlange we bring our story to a close. By what was said during the man's last hours on earth, Mortimer Arbuckle was entirely cleared of the cloud which had hung over his honorable name. Soon after this his right mind came back to him and to-day he is as well and happy as it is possible to imagine.

Whatever became of Stillwater and Juan Donomez is not known.

With the truce declared by the actions of the authorities at Washington and the word given by Pawnee Brown that no attempt should be made to enter Oklahoma for the present, it was not deemed advisable to hold either Dick or Rasco longer, and the two were given their freedom, to journey at once to Honnewell, in company with the great scout and Nellie Winthrop.

From Honnewell, Dick rode post haste to carry the glad news to his father. A scene followed which no pen can describe, a scene so sacred to the two it must be left entirely to the imagination of the reader. Never was a man more proud of his son than was Mortimer Arbuckle of Dick, or more grateful than was the mine-owner to Pawnee Brown for his courageous and marvelous work in clearing up the mystery.

"He is a man among men," he said. "God bless him!"

Nellie Winthrop was overjoyed to be with her uncle once again, and took good care that nothing should separate them. As for Jack, he guarded her with a care which could not be exceeded.

"Ef they carry her off again it will be over my dead body, b'gosh," he murmured more than once.

And yet Nellie was carried off four years later. But this time the carrying off was done by Dick Arbuckle, and both Nellie and Jack were perfectly willing. The wedding was a grand one, for the Colorado claims had panned out big for the Arbuckles, and the best man at the affair was Pawnee Brown.

In due course of time the bill concerning Oklahoma was passed by the United States Senate and signed by the President. This was followed by a grand rush of the boomers to get the best of the land granted to them. The advance was led by

Pawnee Brown, who, riding his ever faithful Bonnie Bird, covered twenty miles in the short space of sixty-five minutes and located his town site at the mouth of Big Turkey Creek. This town site, along with his other Oklahoma possessions, made the great scout a rich man. He never grows weary of telling about this great rush into Oklahoma. "It was grand, awe-inspiring," he says. "I would go a thousand miles to see it again--those hundreds of wagons, thousands of horsemen and heads of cattle, all going southward, over hills, through forests, crossing brooks and rivers--all bound for the land which has since made them so prosperous and happy."

And here let us take leave of Dick Arbuckle, Pawnee Brown, and all their friends, wishing them well.

The Codes Of Hammurabi And Moses
W. W. Davies

QTY

The discovery of the Hammurabi Code is one of the greatest achievements of archaeology, and is of paramount interest, not only to the student of the Bible, but also to all those interested in ancient history...

Religion   **ISBN:** *1-59462-338-4*   **Pages:132**
MSRP $12.95

The Theory of Moral Sentiments
Adam Smith

QTY

This work from 1749. contains original theories of conscience amd moral judgment and it is the foundation for systemof morals.

Philosophy **ISBN:** *1-59462-777-0*   **Pages:536**
MSRP $19.95

Jessica's First Prayer
Hesba Stretton

QTY

In a screened and secluded corner of one of the many railway-bridges which span the streets of London there could be seen a few years ago, from five o'clock every morning until half past eight, a tidily set-out coffee-stall, consisting of a trestle and board, upon which stood two large tin cans, with a small fire of charcoal burning under each so as to keep the coffee boiling during the early hours of the morning when the work-people were thronging into the city on their way to their daily toil...

Pages:84

Childrens   **ISBN:** *1-59462-373-2*   *MSRP $9.95*

My Life and Work
Henry Ford

QTY

Henry Ford revolutionized the world with his implementation of mass production for the Model T automobile. Gain valuable business insight into his life and work with his own auto-biography... "We have only started on our development of our country we have not as yet, with all our talk of wonderful progress, done more than scratch the surface. The progress has been wonderful enough but..."

Pages:300

Biographies/   **ISBN:** *1-59462-198-5*   *MSRP $21.95*

The Art of Cross-Examination
Francis Wellman

QTY

I presume it is the experience of every author, after his first book is published upon an important subject, to be almost overwhelmed with a wealth of ideas and illustrations which could readily have been included in his book, and which to his own mind, at least, seem to make a second edition inevitable. Such certainly was the case with me; and when the first edition had reached its sixth impression in five months, I rejoiced to learn that it seemed to my publishers that the book had met with a sufficiently favorable reception to justify a second and considerably enlarged edition. ..

Reference   ISBN: *1-59462-647-2*

Pages:412

MSRP $19.95

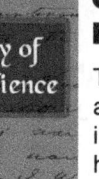

On the Duty of Civil Disobedience
Henry David Thoreau

QTY

Thoreau wrote his famous essay, On the Duty of Civil Disobedience, as a protest against an unjust but popular war and the immoral but popular institution of slave-owning. He did more than write—he declined to pay his taxes, and was hauled off to gaol in consequence. Who can say how much this refusal of his hastened the end of the war and of slavery ?

Law   ISBN: *1-59462-747-9*

Pages:48

MSRP $7.45

Dream Psychology Psychoanalysis for Beginners
Sigmund Freud

QTY

Sigmund Freud, born Sigismund Schlomo Freud (May 6, 1856 - September 23, 1939), was a Jewish-Austrian neurologist and psychiatrist who co-founded the psychoanalytic school of psychology. Freud is best known for his theories of the unconscious mind, especially involving the mechanism of repression; his redefinition of sexual desire as mobile and directed towards a wide variety of objects; and his therapeutic techniques, especially his understanding of transference in the therapeutic relationship and the presumed value of dreams as sources of insight into unconscious desires.

Psychology   ISBN: *1-59462-905-6*

Pages:196

MSRP $15.45

The Miracle of Right Thought
Orison Swett Marden

QTY

Believe with all of your heart that you will do what you were made to do. When the mind has once formed the habit of holding cheerful, happy, prosperous pictures, it will not be easy to form the opposite habit. It does not matter how improbable or how far away this realization may see, or how dark the prospects may be, if we visualize them as best we can, as vividly as possible, hold tenaciously to them and vigorously struggle to attain them, they will gradually become actualized, realized in the life. But a desire, a longing without endeavor, a yearning abandoned or held indifferently will vanish without realization.

Pages:360

Self Help   ISBN: *1-59462-644-8*

MSRP $25.45

www.bookjungle.com *email: sales@bookjungle.com fax: 630-214-0564 mail: Book Jungle PO Box 2226 Champaign, IL 61825*

QTY

The Rosicrucian Cosmo-Conception Mystic Christianity by *Max Heindel* ISBN: *1-59462-188-8* **$38.95**
The Rosicrucian Cosmo-conception is not dogmatic, neither does it appeal to any other authority than the reason of the student. It is: not controversial, but is: sent forth in the, hope that it may help to clear... New Age/Religion Pages 646

Abandonment To Divine Providence by *Jean-Pierre de Caussade* ISBN: *1-59462-228-0* **$25.95**
"The Rev. Jean Pierre de Caussade was one of the most remarkable spiritual writers of the Society of Jesus in France in the 18th Century. His death took place at Toulouse in 1751. His works have gone through many editions and have been republished... Inspirational/Religion Pages 400

Mental Chemistry by *Charles Haanel* ISBN: *1-59462-192-6* **$23.95**
Mental Chemistry allows the change of material conditions by combining and appropriately utilizing the power of the mind. Much like applied chemistry creates something new and unique out of careful combinations of chemicals the mastery of mental chemistry... New Age Pages 354

The Letters of Robert Browning and Elizabeth Barret Barrett 1845-1846 vol II ISBN: *1-59462-193-4* **$35.95**
by *Robert Browning* and *Elizabeth Barrett* Biographies Pages 596

Gleanings In Genesis (volume I) by *Arthur W. Pink* ISBN: *1-59462-130-6* **$27.45**
Appropriately has Genesis been termed "the seed plot of the Bible" for in it we have, in germ form, almost all of the great doctrines which are afterwards fully developed in the books of Scripture which follow... Religion/Inspirational Pages 420

The Master Key by *L. W. de Laurence* ISBN: *1-59462-001-6* **$30.95**
In no branch of human knowledge has there been a more lively increase of the spirit of research during the past few years than in the study of Psychology, Concentration and Mental Discipline. The requests for authentic lessons in Thought Control, Mental Discipline and... New Age/Business Pages 422

The Lesser Key Of Solomon Goetia by *L. W. de Laurence* ISBN: *1-59462-092-X* **$9.95**
This translation of the first book of the "Lerngeton" which is now for the first time made accessible to students of Talismanic Magic was done, after careful collation and edition, from numerous Ancient Manuscripts in Hebrew, Latin, and French... New Age/Occult Pages 92

Rubaiyat Of Omar Khayyam by *Edward Fitzgerald* ISBN:*1-59462-332-5* **$13.95**
Edward Fitzgerald, whom the world has already learned, in spite of his own efforts to remain within the shadow of anonymity, to look upon as one of the rarest poets of the century, was born at Bredfield, in Suffolk, on the 31st of March, 1809. He was the third son of John Purcell... Music Pages 172

Ancient Law by *Henry Maine* ISBN: *1-59462-128-4* **$29.95**
The chief object of the following pages is to indicate some of the earliest ideas of mankind, as they are reflected in Ancient Law, and to point out the relation of those ideas to modern thought. Religion/History Pages 452

Far-Away Stories by *William J. Locke* ISBN: *1-59462-129-2* **$19.45**
"Good wine needs no bush, but a collection of mixed vintages does. And this book is just such a collection. Some of the stories I do not want to remain buried for ever in the museum files of dead magazine-numbers an author's not unpardonable vanity..." Fiction Pages 272

Life of David Crockett by *David Crockett* ISBN: *1-59462-250-7* **$27.45**
"Colonel David Crockett was one of the most remarkable men of the times in which he lived. Born in humble life, but gifted with a strong will, an indomitable courage, and unremitting perseverance... Biographies/New Age Pages 424

Lip-Reading by *Edward Nitchie* ISBN: *1-59462-206-X* **$25.95**
Edward B. Nitchie, founder of the New York School for the Hard of Hearing, now the Nitchie School of Lip-Reading, Inc, wrote "LIP-READING Principles and Practice". The development and perfecting of this meritorious work on lip-reading was an undertaking... How-to Pages 400

A Handbook of Suggestive Therapeutics, Applied Hypnotism, Psychic Science ISBN: *1-59462-214-0* **$24.95**
by *Henry Munro* Health/New Age/Health/Self-help Pages 376

A Doll's House: and Two Other Plays by *Henrik Ibsen* ISBN: *1-59462-112-8* **$19.95**
Henrik Ibsen created this classic when in revolutionary 1848 Rome. Introducing some striking concepts in playwriting for the realist genre, this play has been studied the world over. Fiction/Classics/Plays 308

The Light of Asia by *sir Edwin Arnold* ISBN: *1-59462-204-3* **$13.95**
In this poetic masterpiece, Edwin Arnold describes the life and teachings of Buddha. The man who was to become known as Buddha to the world was born as Prince Gautama of India but he rejected the worldly riches and abandoned the reigns of power when... Religion/History/Biographies Pages 170

The Complete Works of Guy de Maupassant by *Guy de Maupassant* ISBN: *1-59462-157-8* **$16.95**
"For days and days, nights and nights, I had dreamed of that first kiss which was to consecrate our engagement, and I knew not on what spot I should put my lips..." Fiction/Classics Pages 240

The Art of Cross-Examination by *Francis L. Wellman* ISBN: *1-59462-309-0* **$26.95**
Written by a renowned trial lawyer, Wellman imparts his experience and uses case studies to explain how to use psychology to extract desired information through questioning. How-to/Science/Reference Pages 408

Answered or Unanswered? by *Louisa Vaughan* ISBN: *1-59462-248-5* **$10.95**
Miracles of Faith in China Religion Pages 112

The Edinburgh Lectures on Mental Science (1909) by *Thomas* ISBN: *1-59462-008-3* **$11.95**
This book contains the substance of a course of lectures recently given by the writer in the Queen Street Hail, Edinburgh. Its purpose is to indicate the Natural Principles governing the relation between Mental Action and Material Conditions... New Age/Psychology Pages 148

Ayesha by *H. Rider Haggard* ISBN: *1-59462-301-5* **$24.95**
Verily and indeed it is the unexpected that happens! Probably if there was one person upon the earth from whom the Editor of this, and of a certain previous history, did not expect to hear again... Classics Pages 380

Ayala's Angel by *Anthony Trollope* ISBN: *1-59462-352-X* **$29.95**
The two girls were both pretty, but Lucy who was twenty-one who supposed to be simple and comparatively unattractive, whereas Ayala was credited, as her Bombwhat romantic name might show, with poetic charm and a taste for romance. Ayala when her father died was nineteen... Fiction Pages 484

The American Commonwealth by *James Bryce* ISBN: *1-59462-286-8* **$34.45**
An interpretation of American democratic political theory. It examines political mechanics and society from the perspective of Scotsman James Bryce Politics Pages 572

Stories of the Pilgrims by *Margaret P. Pumphrey* ISBN: *1-59462-116-0* **$17.95**
This book explores pilgrims religious oppression in England as well as their escape to Holland and eventual crossing to America on the Mayflower, and their early days in New England... History Pages 268

QTY

The Fasting Cure *by Sinclair Upton*
In the Cosmopolitan Magazine for May, 1910, and in the Contemporary Review (London) for April, 1910, I published an article dealing with my experiences in fasting. I have written a great many magazine articles, but never one which attracted so much attention... ISBN: *1-59462-222-1* **$13.95**
New Age/Self Help/Health Pages 164

Hebrew Astrology *by Sepharial*
In these days of advanced thinking it is a matter of common observation that we have left many of the old landmarks behind and that we are now pressing forward to greater heights and to a wider horizon than that which represented the mind-content of our progenitors... ISBN: *1-59462-308-2* **$13.45**
Astrology Pages 144

Thought Vibration or The Law of Attraction in the Thought World
by William Walker Atkinson ISBN: *1-59462-127-6* **$12.95**
Psychology/Religion Pages 144

Optimism *by Helen Keller*
Helen Keller was blind, deaf, and mute since 19 months old, yet famously learned how to overcome these handicaps, communicate with the world, and spread her lectures promoting optimism. An inspiring read for everyone... ISBN: *1-59462-108-X* **$15.95**
Biographies/Inspirational Pages 84

Sara Crewe *by Frances Burnett*
In the first place, Miss Minchin lived in London. Her home was a large, dull, tall one, in a large, dull square, where all the houses were alike, and all the sparrows were alike, and where all the door-knockers made the same heavy sound... ISBN: *1-59462-360-0* **$9.45**
Childrens/Classic Pages 88

The Autobiography of Benjamin Franklin *by Benjamin Franklin*
The Autobiography of Benjamin Franklin has probably been more extensively read than any other American historical work, and no other book of its kind has had such ups and downs of fortune. Franklin lived for many years in England, where he was agent... ISBN: *1-59462-135-7* **$24.95**
Biographies/History Pages 332

Name	
Email	
Telephone	
Address	
City, State ZIP	

☐ **Credit Card**   ☐ **Check / Money Order**

Credit Card Number	
Expiration Date	
Signature	

Please Mail to: Book Jungle
PO Box 2226
Champaign, IL 61825
or Fax to: 630-214-0564

ORDERING INFORMATION
web*: www.bookjungle.com*
email*: sales@bookjungle.com*
fax*: 630-214-0564*
mail*: Book Jungle PO Box 2226 Champaign, IL 61825*
or PayPal *to sales@bookjungle.com*

Please contact us for bulk discounts

DIRECT-ORDER TERMS

**20% Discount if You Order
Two or More Books**
Free Domestic Shipping!
Accepted: Master Card, Visa,
Discover, American Express